eleven weeks

eleven weeks

crazy in love #2

Lauren K. McKellar

ISBN: 978-0-9924524-3-8 (print)

Cover copyright © K. A. Last of KILA Designs
www.kiladesigns.com.au
Editing by Marion Archer of Marion's Making Manuscripts
www.makingmanuscripts.com
Editorial Formatting by Tianne Samson with E.M. Tippetts Book Designs
www.emtippettsbookdesigns.com

BOOKS BY LAUREN K. MCKELLAR

Finding Home

Crazy In Love Series

The Problem With Crazy
Eleven Weeks
The Problem With Heartache

*For my mother, because you really are there when I need you
(and no, don't worry, I don't think you're Stacey's mum) x*

week one

November 12

WAKE TO the sound of a drill-saw attempting to channel through a concrete pylon right next to my head.

"Why?" I grunt. Only it sounds more like "arrggghhh", even to my ears. Apparently being woken by a drill-saw seriously impedes my ability to form words. I reach my hand out and slam something in front of me, presumably the drill-saw, most likely a clock radio. Regardless, the action makes the noise stop. Thank hell.

Ugh. While the blast of noise has stopped, there's still a ringing in my head of dizzy-making proportions. Not to mention that my tongue tastes like I've been eating road kill. Yuck.

I squint one eye open and then scrunch my lid shut immediately. Harsh yellow light screams through a window framed by black, floral curtains. What fresh hell is this? Who has opened my—

Shit.

I don't have black, floral curtains.

I inch open my lid at a snail's pace, this time preparing

myself for the assault of light from the left of the room. Yep. Black, floral curtains still there.

I open my eyes wider and take in more of the room in front of me. Aside from the window, there's a black bedside table with a digital clock on the top of it, right next to a red lamp. The floor is covered in a shaggy cream carpet, with a black skirt and a red lacy bra lying on top of it.

Oh, no. Please, please no …

I slowly raise the white sheet from my body. Yep, exactly as I'd suspected.

My black skirt and red bra.

This, of course, leaves only one question. But do I really want to look? Can I?

I rack my brain, trying to put together the pieces of the night before. There was the party at Joe's. I'd gone there with Kate, because Dave and the band were playing. Michael. I saw Michael. Tequila. *Lots* of tequila.

I glanced down at my hand. Seven little lipstick lines mar its surface. One for each shot. At least I can remember that.

But how the hell did I get here? And, more importantly, *where is here?*

With my body still firmly positioned toward the left side of the room, I gently inch my foot behind me.

One inch: nothing. Just cool, crisp sheet.

Two inches: still nothing.

Three inches: so far, so good. Hopefully I'm alone. I just went to some stranger's house, took off all my clothes, and slept solo in a random bed.

Four in—*shit!* My big toe makes contact with something warm, hairy, and distinctively human. I jerk my leg back toward me. My heart thuds in my chest, a million miles a minute. What the hell have I done? And who am I in bed with?

My mind races through the potential options. Grant, my ex, hadn't been at the party, and he sure as hell didn't have black, flowered curtains. There had been Joe, the older guy whose place the party was at. He'd definitely shown an interest in me, in particular when I'd told him I was eighteen tomorrow.

Today. Technically, I am eighteen right now.

"Hoooaaaawwwwr." The creature behind me groan-yawns.

It's like a bullet from a starter gun. I fling the sheets back and jump from the bed. I dive for my clothes, pulling on my underwear, throwing my shirt over my head and hoisting up my skirt like this is the Olympic event for sprint-dressing and I'm the lead contestant.

I grab my bra from the floor and thank the god of hangovers that my mobile is hidden underneath it, along with my flip-flops, which I promptly slip on.

"Hey," a deep voice calls from behind me. A voice I don't really recognise. It sounds like a million male voices, all rolled into one.

I freeze. Is it better to know and deal with it, or run and hide in shame?

Only there's not really a question.

I'll take the shame, thanks, my legs tell my brain as they sprint toward the door. I wrench it open and then slam it shut behind me, the mystery man calling something in my wake.

I'm in a living room with black leather lounges in front of me, and a giant flat-screen TV to the left. Windows with more of those hideous curtains let in cruel, natural light and next to them—*thank you, thank you, thank you*—a door, the kind of thick, wooden thing that clearly screams *exit*.

I dart toward it, screeching as I step on some small, sharp, red object in my path, twist the door handle, and then run out into the street. I slam it shut behind me and run, run down past the trees, the gravel of the unsealed road digging into my feet.

I run until my breath comes in short, sharp gasps that make my chest shudder. I run until water seeps from the corners of my eyes, streaking out past my temples, no doubt giving me that desirable panda effect.

I turn left, I run; I turn right, I run. I go straight through several intersections until the stitch in my side is stabbing and the throbbing in my head, merciless. I double over and rest my hands on my knees, trying to slow my breathing, to gain some semblance of control over my body. I have no idea where I am. I have no idea where I've been.

"One," I whisper, holding my breath for the imaginary *one thousand*. "Two." *One thousand*. "Three." *One thousand*.

By the time I reach ten, my breathing is a distant cousin of normal, and I straighten up and try to think again.

I dial Kate's number, but she doesn't pick up. I think about calling a taxi, but I don't have my purse on me, and what would I say, anyway? Please pick me up from number four I-Have-No-Freaking-Clue Street? Do you accept pretend payment?

Think, Stacey, think. I massage my temple with my left hand, my right still clutching my phone and bra.

Noise. Head toward traffic, then you can work out what street you're on, and try figure a way to get home.

I shut my eyes and concentrate on the noises around me. The chirping of birds—not helping. Traffic. The sound of cars, yes. Coming from … from the right. Yes. The right.

I pick up my pace, trying to ball my bra into a fist-sized package. The underwire makes it a little difficult, and for the first time in my life I curse myself for buying a bra that's sexy instead of practical. Seconds later, I banish the thought from my brain and send up a mental apology to La Perla for ever thinking that way.

Still, it gets me thinking. Sexy lingerie. Something I wore in the hope someone would see it and now, judging by all the things that have happened so far this morning (read: naked wake-up call, strange man in bed next to me, slight ache between my legs, and lips that feel a little bee-stung, potentially from too much kissing from a guy who possesses a great deal of chin stubble), yes, someone did.

Did we even use protection?

My stomach swells and a surge of bile makes its way up my throat, rolling into my mouth. I double over and swallow it down, determined not to vomit in some random person's rose bush. I may be hungover and doing the walk of shame—well, in my case, run of shame—but there is no reason I can't have standards.

The rumble of an engine working its way down the street has me jumping over to the footpath to avoid imminent death. *Nothing worse than having a one-night stand with a mystery guy and then being run over, on your birthday …*

The engine slows down, chugging along behind me. I keep my eyes firmly fixed on the pavement, my pace fierce.

Still, the car moves along just behind me. My heart, which had slowed from the excessive running, starts to pick up again, building to a march. Is someone following me? Who?

What if it's the guy from the house?

Rationally, I know the thought shouldn't scare me. This guy has seen me naked.

What if it's someone else?

I mentally change my list from having a one-night stand with a mystery guy and getting run over on your birthday as being the least impressive annual occasion ever, and replace getting run over with being stalked, kidnapped, and chopped up into tiny pieces.

Yep. Not panicking.

Frick!

I insert a small skip into my step, trying to seem as casual as an eighteen-year-old girl skipping can be. The car keeps pace just behind me.

My eyes scan the street till I see a small alley three buildings away. I could run down there. The car won't be able to follow me. And the lane is even leading to my right, toward the sound of cars and hopefully familiarity.

I take a quick glance to my left—safety first—when the car engine stops.

It just *stops*.

Damn.

Before I can run, though, I hear my name. "Stacey."

I spin around. The car following me is an old mint-green Valiant. And the guy sticking his head out the window I know only too well.

"Michael." I give a rueful smile and turn my head away. I

don't know if the fact I know him makes this better or worse.

"Whatcha doing?" he asks.

Oh you know, just the walk of shame home from a guy's house, one who I probably slept with and who, judging from the ache between my legs, I'd say has a medium to sightly above average-sized penis.

"You know, nothing much." I shrug.

Michael furrows his brow, and his gaze lowers to my—*oh my God I am not wearing a bra!* I cross my arms over my chest, hoping like hell he can't see my nipples. He grins.

He can totally see my nipples.

His brown hair is pulled back in a knot behind his head, his eyes fresh as bloody daisies. I could have sworn he'd had shots last night, too …

"How come you look so chipper?"

"Chipper?"

"Like, not hungover," I clarify.

"Maybe because while I did take my top off on-stage last night, I did it after two shots of tequila, not seven?"

Oh. Did that mean I …?

"The look on your face." Michael laughs softly.

I huff out a breath and narrow my eyes. "See ya." I flip him the bird and keep walking. Like I need anyone else making me feel like crap today. I've done a fine job of that myself.

"Wait! Wait." The car door squeaks open and Michael's feet thud behind me, then his hand is on my shoulder. It's a warm hand. Big. Steady. "I'm sorry, Stace."

"Yeah, whatever." I shrug him off.

"Hey, I mean it." He spins me round to face him. His deep, brown eyes aren't mocking; they just appear concerned. "Can I give you a ride?"

I look back at his car. I know being in a confined space with this guy isn't a good idea, but desperate times call for desperate measures.

"Thanks," I mumble. He leads me back to the vehicle, opening the passenger-side door with a grand flourish, then slides over the bonnet and jumps in the driver's seat. Seconds later, we're pulling out from the curb, heading toward the direction I'd thought was the main part of town.

The car smells like McDonald's wrappers and male body odour, no doubt not just Michael's, but also his other band buddies', too. Papers litter the floor at my feet, and a collection of six empty coffee cups, all stacked into one another, litter the two-hole cup-holder.

I blink, and the second my eyes close an image flashes into my mind: voices yelling at the party. *Vodka. Tequila. Beer. Lips I don't recognise pressing against my own.*

Ugh.

"I love this song." Michael leans forward and swivels the dial on the radio. I swallow down my guilt. A track by the Rolling Stones blares out of the car's crackly speakers, a song about sinners and saints.

Two guesses which of those I feel like today …

We reach the main part of town in quite a short time. It's crazy how I'd been so close, yet so far away; I guess that's the beauty of suburbia. Everything can look the same, sound the same, despite the subtle Stepford Wives-style differences.

"So, you had fun last night?" Michael asks, not taking his eyes off the road, which I appreciate. I'm a terrible backseat driver.

"Mmhmm," I reply. "You?"

"It was amazing. Best night, Stace." He looks at me again, and this time the wheel swings along with his gaze. The car bumps the gutter and I grab the door as Michael gives a quick shake of his head and swerves back to the road.

"Amazing? Why? Something special happen?" I tilt my head, letting my gaze flick from the road to Michael, then back to the road again. His face is etched in concentration as he bites his lip. I can't help but stare at them for a moment.

Unfamiliar lips.

I swallow down the sick still lurking in my throat. Why did I drink so much?

"Well, I just … I don't know. I mean, it was fine, I guess. You don't … remember anything about it?"

Isn't that the million-dollar question?

"Just you and the band sounding great," I try, flashing him what I hope is a convincing smile.

"Nothing else?" He narrows his eyes.

"Oh, you know. Just the usual party stuff."

"Huh."

Crap.

"Tell me, what'd I do? Did I make an idiot of myself?" I grab at Michael's shirt and he looks at me, then jerks the wheel back to the right to avoid us running into a little old lady who is taking out her recycling bin.

"It's … nothing."

But his face says it's everything.

Seconds later he shakes his head, as if he were shaking away some bad thought. "So what are our plans for today?"

"Huh?" I'm starting to sound like a broken record.

"Today. Your birthday." He speaks the words slowly, like I am a small child.

My birthday? How the hell did he remember that?

"You … remembered?"

"Stacey, we've known each other since the start of high school." Michael sighs. "Of course I remembered."

He does have a point. I furrow my brows, trying to remember when his birthday is.

"June?"

He doesn't so much as hesitate. The damn bastard knows exactly what I'm on about. "Not even close."

"January?"

"Uh-uh." Michael gives a wicked grin. "It's not a competition. Anyway, what are we doing to celebrate?"

"I was just going to have dinner with my family …" *After I go home and try and scrape the sluttiness off me.*

"Right." Michael nods. Only, instead of turning right, as he'd been indicating and waiting at the lights to do, he swerves back into the traffic, going straight ahead. My heart lurches and I tighten my grip on the door.

"Michael?"

"Yeah?" He flicks me a quick glance.

"Where are we going?"

"Birthday stuff." He smiles. His lips curve up, dimples crease both his cheeks, and it's so hard for me to ignore the little flames sparking in my belly. Stupid, idiotic Stacey. This is Michael. And he isn't interested.

I smile and gaze out the window as we drive. We leave the roads of the city and head out to the streets that lead to the cliff-tops. Michael's car chugs along, The Beatles blaring out the radio now as we cruise past green grassy knolls, sheer cliff face, and wide, blue ocean, with specks of white flaring up in the wind.

It's so beautiful out there—the sun shining down, highlighting the bold colours—that I can't help it. I wind down the window—a full-body activity, no doubt due to the age of the car—and shove my head and shoulders out of the car. The wind whips my face, stripping away the shame and embarrassment I felt after my activities the night before. This is so real.

This is free.

I let the cool sea breeze flick my hair behind me and lick my lips, the faint taste of salt playing in my mouth. My lids slowly shut as I tilt my head up toward the sun's rays. For one moment, I'm alive.

"You're …"

My eyes fly open and I pull myself back into the car, turning to Michael, a grin on my face. "Yeah?"

Silence stretches out between us, as wide as the ocean in the distance.

"Nothing."

I turn my head back out the window and give a sly smile. I don't know what "I" am, but I like the way he said it. Even if I know I shouldn't.

We pull over in the seaside village, lined with touristy shops. This is the place where people come to holiday, and the local businesses reflect that, with the overpriced clothing boutiques, fancy day spas, and fish-and-chip shops where you can choose between grilled with herb butter or stuffed with frog's legs or something, instead of just your usual battered or fried.

Michael pulls the car to the curb and switches the engine off. He unhitches his seatbelt and runs around to my side of the car to fling open the door before I can so much as undo my own restraint.

"Thanks." I smile up at him. His eyes gleam.

I stand and hop out of the car after stuffing my bra in a corner on the floor but taking my phone with me. Something warm stirs in my stomach, and I try hard to push it down. I've pretended like this for years. What's one more day?

The sick feeling rises again. Bile claws at my throat.

"Are you okay?" Michael places his hand on my lower back. I double over, grabbing my stomach one more time and fight the wave of sickness that attempts to battle its way out of my mouth. Swallowing it down is so very acidic and disgusting, but spewing in broad daylight in front of hundreds of tourists—some of whom could be hot—is undoubtedly worse.

"Fine." I straighten myself up.

"You look …" Michael pauses, and his eyes focus on my face. He jerks back his hand from behind me, as if he's been caught stealing lollies from a jar. "… pale."

"I'm fine."

"Okay." Michael starts walking toward the beach, already packed with tourists, despite the cool spring breeze. I race to follow, practically tripping over my feet in the effort. He passes the flags and heads toward the rocks, where a couple canoodles in the sand.

"Romantic." I nod in their direction.

Michael turns the colour of a beetroot.

"Jokes." I elbow his side and he shakes his head and gives a weird laugh, casting me with *that look* again, the one he started when he asked me what I remembered about last night.

"I'll be right back." He turns away.

"Huh?" I fold my arms. "You're leaving me?"

"Give me three minutes." He holds up three fingers in the air, then bolts down the beach, leaping off the last rock and flying over the sand, heading back up toward the main drag.

I shrug and settle myself down on a flat rock. The ocean is calmer here, the wind not whipping up the waves due to protection from the cliff face. The waves crash down onto the sand farther to my left and I close my eyes and rest back on my elbows, enjoying the feeling of being by the sea, of being alive.

I'm eighteen. I screwed up last night, sure, but it's not like I've never made a mistake before. Besides, things are going to change.

Change. I shiver at the thought. Everyone else has been so freaking excited about school ending in a few weeks.

All I feel is dread.

Being social is perhaps the only thing I'm good at.

My mind flashes back to the night before once more. Seven shots of tequila. One night of presumably drunken sex with a total stranger.

I bite my lip till I taste blood. That was low, even for me.

I press my thighs together again. That unwelcome burn stings me again. I bury my face in my hands. *What was I thinking?*

"Happy birthday."

I turn to my left to see Michael scrambling over the rocks toward me. In his hands, he holds two plastic bags.

He sits down next to me. "Close your eyes."

Normally, I wouldn't be so quick to acquiesce, but this is Michael—*my* Michael, who I'm about to watch walk out of my life.

I obediently scrunch my eyes tight. The rustling of paper and plastic mixes together, followed by a flare of energy, and then the distinct acrid scent that can only be attributed to a match burning.

"Happy birthday to you ..." Michael sings.

I open my eyes. In front of us, balanced on a higher rock, are two bacon and egg rolls, one with five candles jammed into the doughy surface, all alight. "Happy birthday dear Stacey ..."

God, I must have had a big night. Those can't be tears in my eyes, can they?

"Happy birthday to you."

I blink, and turn to look at him. He's smiling, the sort of ear-to-ear grin that just melts your heart. I open my mouth to speak, but I choke on the words; they're stuck in my throat. What I really want to say is, *why would you do this for me?* But all I vocalise is "thank you."

"Blow the candles out." He dips his head toward my bacon and egg cake, and I obediently suck in a deep breath and blow. Five little lights wink out, and I grin.

"Now, if your teeth cut through the roll, I think you have to kiss the closest boy?" Michael asks, biting his lip.

I don't know if I'm still drunk from the night prior, or if perhaps I'm just so hungover that the simplest of gestures has managed to make me way too emotional. All I know is that one moment I'm giggling, and the next I'm leaning over and kissing Michael on the cheek.

It's quick, barely longer than a peck. And purely to show my appreciation for all the effort he has gone to.

But he smells of clean, of fresh linen, but with a little bit of man mixed in. And his eyes, have they always been so flecked with gold?

"Thank you." I pull away, duck my head, then reach over to grab my roll.

Silence stretches out between us, but I can't make conversation right now. Not when the scent of bacon is slowly healing my soul.

I take a big bite, relishing in the yolk that explodes in my mouth, meshing with the bread and the bacon, covering the taste of something akin to blue cheese gone bad that had previously been getting busy on my tongue.

Bite number two and some sauce squirts down my chin. I swipe it away with my knuckles then go for bite three, freezing when I feel Michael's gaze on me.

"What?" I ask. He doesn't waver, focusing on my face. "Haven't you ever seen anyone eat a bacon and egg roll before?"

"You …" He bites his lip. Then he leans forward, reaches out his hand and cups my chin, using his thumb to gently wipe the corner of my lip.

I swallow. He's so close to me—his face, his body, his breath. My eyes meet his and get lost once more. He bought me a birthday bacon and egg roll. And he's always been such a sweetheart …

But he's Michael. *In-a-band, soon-to-have-groupies, likes-to-tease-you-and-say-you're-pretty-but-has-never-expressed-real-interest* Michael. Michael who, up until two months ago, was in a relationship. One that lasted for two years.

Michael, who I've pretended not to love for as long as I've known him.

"You know, Stacey. I kind of like … like …" He swallows.

I give a playful swipe with my hand and push Michael away from my face. I focus my gaze back on my roll. Egg and sauce are oozing out of its middle, pus-like liquid that churns my stomach.

A flash of last night comes back to me. *Sauce, oozing out of a burger. A tongue, oozing out of* his *mouth.* Bile churns up my throat again, and I somehow swallow it down.

"Stace? You okay?" Michael's concerned expression breaks my reverie and I snap back to the present. To the now.

To my eighteenth birthday. With Michael.

"Fine." I give a wan smile and attempt another half-hearted bite of my roll, but for me, the magic is gone. I crumple up the paper around the bread and offer what I hope is a non-bitchy smile. "Mind if we head? I'm kinda tired."

"Sure." Michael shrugs and stands up, brushing off his jeans. He pauses, then holds out one hand for me, and I gratefully use it to help myself to my feet.

We walk to the car in silence. I follow in his footsteps, trying to fit my tiny feet into the marks he leaves in the sand, one for one. Like having that tiny sense of connection with another human being will ease the pain of the irresponsible lunacy I committed last night.

He doesn't know. No one has to know.

When we reach the car, Michael holds the door open for me with a flourish. "Your seat, *mademoiselle*."

"Do you even speak French?" I ask, resting against the cool metal of the fence behind me.

"Depends." Michael swaggers closer to me, till there are just a few inches separating our bodies. My breath hitches in my throat. He's so close. So close I can smell the salt and the fresh scent of him. His stubbled throat gleams, and I have this weird desire to lick it.

"Depends on who I need to impress with the language of love."

At that, I roll my eyes once more. And that's the crux of it. No matter how much I crush on Michael, he's never going to take me seriously. Just like the rest of Lakes, he sees me as a piece of freaking ass. Someone he's always flirted with, even when he had a girlfriend. Some blonde bimbo.

"Thank God I speak the language of hangover, and know that all those who use terms like 'language of love' are usually douchebags." I shoulder past Michael and slide my way toward the seat, only he reaches for my side and pulls me flush up against him. His body is close to mine, his breath warm on my neck, my cheek … my mouth.

"We …" I don't even know what I'm about to say. All I know is that this moment is here, and I feel like I'm coming home. Like I've wanted this my whole life, but I've known it's something I could never have. It's like indulging in chocolate cake, and deciding to start the diet tomorrow.

Then Michael steps back. It's like a slap in the face. It's like a needle in the eye.

"Is everything … okay?" I bite my lip. His eyes aren't focused on mine anymore. They're centred behind me, on the car floor.

I spin around, searching for the possible reason for Michael's distraction, and I see it. My black and red lacy bra where I'd left it, fully exposed, thanks to the open car door.

"You didn't … you didn't go home last night, did you?" Michael's voice is soft, his face pale. He already knows. And I think I knew this was coming from the moment I hopped in his car.

I want nothing more than to tell him sweet nothings. *No, of course not, I always find my way back. I stayed at a friend's place, and forgot to put my underwear on after the shower.*

That? Oh, that. I, uh, left the house in such a rush at my shock of being SUCH a skank that I forgot to put it on.

Neither of those scream *perfect alibi* to me.

"No." I swallow. A little light, a fleck of gold in Michael's eyes goes out.

He walks around to his side of the car and opens the door, sliding inside and slamming the door shut with an almighty *thunk* behind him. I lower myself into my seat, pulling the door to and grabbing the offending lingerie from the floor, then stuffing it into my chest.

It doesn't matter. Hell, I've always known that Michael and me? We could never be anything. What's the point when he's in a band that's about to tour the country? What's the point when he flirts but never makes a move?

What's the point when I am nothing?

I blank my subconscious and instead focus on the present. Screw that.

Ten minutes later, we pull up out the front of my house. The only words we've exchanged since the beach are "Left here, thanks" and "Which way now?"

"Thank you." I unclick my belt button and push the door open, sticking one long leg out of it.

"No biggy." Michael shrugs.

"But that's just it." I lean forward. "It's 'no biggy' now, but I know it's a goddamn biggy."

Electricity crackles between us. I look at his lips, imagining how they'd feel on mine.

There's an interminable pause. His eyes flick to my lips, back to my eyes, down to my lips, back to my eyes, as each time he gets progressively closer to my mouth.

"Look, I just think it's not very cool you obviously slept at some dude's house last night," Michael starts.

"It was a girlfriend," I protest, fists on my knees.

"Yeah?" Michael's brow creases. "Like, a girlfriend whose house you slept at without a bra on?"

"Heaps of girls do that." *Don't they?*

"Then how do you explain the hickey on your neck?"

I don't have to reach my hand to feel it. As soon as the words leave his mouth, a sting bites the nape of my neck and an inconsolable burning takes up residence in my cheeks. Flashes of last night come back to me again. *His tongue, lapping at my earlobe. His lips, sucking at my neck.*

No face.

No name.

"Anyway, I should be going." I smile a weak smile.

"Whatever."

It's only one word, but it breaks me. With it, I see the light fade completely from his eyes, the alertness from his posture slump to nothing.

I slam the door shut to the tune of his engine kicking over.

And this is exactly why getting in the car with Michael was a bad idea. Because no matter how hard I try to pretend, he always manages to make me feel empty. He is a good, genuine guy, the kind who is friends with everyone, who plays football, is in a band, and volunteers at our local Meals on Wheels shelter on Sundays.

I cheerlead. I act. The only thing I seem to be good at is pretending.

And I will never be enough.

He drives away and I will him to look back. Something. Anything, just to prove that maybe he cares, that maybe he'd be willing to try and make this work, and that his occasional jokes about my looks, or wanting to kiss me are real. Are more than jokes.

He doesn't look back.

Not even once.

I run inside, quickly shower, and then head back out, grabbing my wallet and keys. I pass Mum on the way. She's in the kitchen chatting with Scott, and I give them a frantic *hi-bye* as I bolt out the door. They don't mention my birthday, but I figure we'll talk about it later. Hell, right now I have more pressing issues—such as, ensuring I don't have to remember a birthday for my unborn baby—to sort out.

Ten minutes later, I've pulled up at the local chemist.

Downside Number 362 of living in a small-ish town: The local pharmacist knows your name.

I peek out from behind a rack of sunscreen. A chick maybe three years older than me occupies the desk behind the prescriptions counter. Mr Holden, my mum's tennis partner's husband, is nowhere in sight.

Thank God.

I inch a leg out from behind the sunscreen stand and start the ultimate ninja sprint toward the prescription counter. I've never not used a condom before. I'm fairly sure that, no matter how boozed I was, I would have insisted upon it.

But since I can't remember going home, having sex, or the guy in question, I figure it's better safe than sorry.

I'm running the gauntlet, dodging shopping baskets, promotional lipstick displays, and small children crawling on the floor.

I slam my hands down on the prescriptions counter. "Excuse me," I say, suddenly breathless. The girl turns to face me. "I need to—"

"Stacey!" I spin around. Mr Holden is standing right behind me. "How are you?"

"Fine." I swallow. Totally, not-even-here-to-take-the-morning-after-pill-and-prevent-potential-pregnancy fine.

"Good. Can I help you?" He squints and stretches his long, skinny frame. He reminds me of a weird stick insect. Always has, always will.

"Ah … I was feeling … sick …" Not a lie. "And I wanted some … thing."

"What kind of symptoms are you presenting, Stacey?" Mr Holden asks, folding his arms across his chest.

Twenty minutes later, after I described my no doubt

mystifying and yet not completely made-up symptoms of a pounding head, nauseous stomach, dry lips and sore throat, I left the chemist with a variety of drugs, from cold and flu tablets to Chapstick.

Not the morning-after pill.

Oops.

I drive for forty minutes and finally find a shop where I don't recognise any of the pharmacy staff. *Thank God.* I guess that's the disadvantage of regional towns; the odds of you knowing everybody are pretty damn high.

Foot in front of hesitant foot, I walk up to the counter to be greeted by a woman who looks just like she could play Mary Poppins in the musical of the same name. Or maybe I'm thinking of the "Raindrops and roses, whiskers on kittens" chick. Either/or.

"Hi, I would like to, uh …" I clasp my hands together, so tight I'm marginally concerned they'll merge into each other.

"Yes?" She nods, her eyes alive.

"Get-the-morning-after-pill-please," I spit out, all as one word.

"Right." She stops spewing rainbows and starts sending me vibes akin to what she would have if someone interrupted her *Eidelweiss*. "Right this way, please."

She gestures to a seat over to the side of the counter, and I take heavy steps over to it.

"The pharmacist will be with you shortly." She gives a curt nod, and departs for behind the desk, where I see her whispering to a tall and very distinguished looking pharmacist. She points, and raises her eyebrows, and I think she even smirks at some point. *You can't trust those nuns …*

The pharmacist takes six long strides over from the counter and stops in front of me. "Hello, Miss …"

"Allison." I nod. "Stacey Allison."

"Right, nice to meet you." He holds out his hand, and I reach over to clasp mine in his, pumping it up and down with confidence.

His forehead creases with confusion, and he tilts his head to the side. "Take a seat?" he asks, as the realisation sets in. He was gesturing to the chair. Not initiating a handshake gesture. *Awkward.*

I lower myself and sit in what could possibly be the world's least comfortable plastic chair. Perhaps this is just another reminder to the kiddies. Don't have unprotected sex. Look where they might make you sit.

"You're here for the morning-after pill," the pharmacist says, scribbling something down on a notepad in front of him.

"Yes," I say. "Please." *Manners, Stacey ...*

"Did you have unprotected sex?" He all but lowers his glasses to give me the full father-effect glare, and I shrink back against the unyielding green plastic.

"I ... I don't actually know." I shrug. What else can I do?

"You don't ... know." He frowns.

"I had too much to drink and sadly, I don't remember the event."

Even as I say the words, the reality of what I've done hits home. Yes, people drink. People drink all the time. But to the point of forgetting? To the point of going home with a stranger, when you're only just knocking on the door of legal drinking age?

My stomach roils and I feel sick again. What the hell was I thinking? This is not the solution to my *how the hell will I cope with life stuck in this stupid town* problem.

"Are you over eighteen?" The pharmacist squints at me, and it makes perfect sense, because right now I'm an amoeba. Less than that, even.

"Yes, I am, actually." I picture my license in my head. Thank goodness I finally am legally allowed to drink. "And, I should add, this is the first time I've ever drunk so much I don't really remember details, and the first time I may have had unprotected sex."

And that is true.

And even though I don't remember things like, say, *who the hell took me home last night*, I do remember other things.

The party. Michael, strumming his bass on stage. The seven tequila shots.

One kiss, scorching my neck.

Two hands, pulling me closer.

Too close.

"So you could have had unprotected sex, and you're taking the pill to be sure," the pharmacist continues, as if I'm not flaying myself with whips of remorse.

"Yes." I nod. I seem to be doing a lot of that lately.

"Are you on any other form of birth control, or do you have any other medication you are currently taking?" he asks, after scribbling a few notes down on the piece of paper in front of him. I shake my head. "And this wasn't your first sexual experience?"

Six very vehement head shakes to that.

"Have you had a pap smear before?" This time, the pharmacist lowers his voice, and I'm almost not sure who is more embarrassed here—him, or me.

I dart my gaze to the corners of the room. Two pensioners, one middle-aged mum and a kid. *Thank God.* "Once."

It's only a little lie. How's he going to know?

"I'm going to give you the morning-after pills to … ahem … minimise the risk of—"

"Whoa, whoa, what do you mean *minimise*?" I narrow my eyes.

"The morning-after pill is only ever eighty-five per cent effective."

I swallow. *Fifteen per cent, hey …*

"However, I would recommend that you see a doctor"—I give a sharp intake of breath—"*today* and get some STD checks done, too."

I suck in a deep breath through my nose. Part of me wants to ignore him, but a larger part doesn't want to risk it. Whether I like it or not, I'm stuck living in this town. And if I do have some weird freaking disease transmitted by Guy I Don't Remember, I'd rather know what it is. So I can get rid of it. And keep it under wraps.

"Cool. Sounds good." I smile. And I nod. Because, der.

"Right. Just wait here a minute, and please fill out this form." The doctor pushes a piece of paper toward me with some basic admin questions and I scribble my details across it, barely checking it twice.

Minutes later, he returns with a small white box, and the same attitude he possessed when he walked over the first time. I'm fairly sure Mary Poppins has turned up her nose.

"Right, this is your—"

But it doesn't matter what else he says. All that matters is that Michael, *my* Michael, is walking into the pharmacy.

Frick.

"Thanks so much." I snatch the box out of his hands and stuff it into my handbag.

"You pay up front." The pharmacist furrows his brows, and tilts his head toward the counter.

"Yes, and I will. Just, you know …" I trail off. You know, what? You know, how embarrassing it is when the guy you have crushed on your entire life, who thinks you may have spent the night with someone else last night, walks into a pharmacy while you're getting the morning-after pill? *You know, that?*

The pharmacist swallows. I keep my gaze fixed on him. "There are two pills. You can take them both together, or, if you're concerned about nausea, we recommend taking them twelve hours apart." My stomach lurches. I'm concerned about nausea, all right. "It has to be noted, though, that you do need to take both. If you do not …" The pharmacist keeps on talking, but I glance behind one more time to see if I can spot Michael. He's looking at sunscreen, picking one bottle up, putting it down. The next bottle up, putting it down … what for? Summer holidays, tour …?

Focus, Stacey.

"And therefore the percentage rate would be less effective. The same goes if you have any health issues, such as vomiting, or diarrhoea, post taking the pill. This can render it less effective." This time, the pharmacist glances over to Michael.

"Should I be directing this talk to him …?"

"No!" My eyes widen, my heart sprinting at a dance-party rate. "No. I got this. Take the pills, twelve hours apart. Go to doctor, have people swab at vagina. Anything else?"

The pharmacist fixes me with a glare that can only be described as *screw you*. "Yes. Don't drink so much."

I'd love to argue, but the guy has a point.

"Stacey!" Michael says my name, and I spin around.

"Michael, hey." I smile, stepping away from the pharmacy counter and closer in to him. As soon as I do, I'm hit by that freaking scent again. Gosh, why does he have to smell so *good*?

"What are you up to?" he asks, at the same time as I say, "What are you doing here?" Because seriously, what is he doing so far from home?

"I had to get some new guitar strings, and the music shop here is so much better than the one near home." He's smiling, and it doesn't feel like the venom, the anger that was in his voice earlier, is still there. Instead, he seems genuinely happy to see me. *Odd.* "What are you here for?"

"Oh, you know …" I shrug, and look around. "Girl things."

Michael's cheeks flush red, then he swallows, and they regain a semblance of their normal colour. Gotta love *girl things*. Best. Line. Ever.

"So, about before—"

"I wanted to say—"

We both look at each other.

"You go first." I smile, lips pressed tight.

"I'm sorry if I didn't believe you." Michael runs his hand through his hair. "I think, the thing is, I was just hating the idea of you being with some random guy so much. I just … Phew!" He widens his eyes, and I can't help but catch his contagious smile. "I just … after what we spoke about last night, I thought you'd just … betrayed me."

There. That look of belief. That look of honesty.

I feel like I've killed a puppy dog.

I've murdered a dream I don't remember.

"No," I rush out. "I mean … you know I don't remember

what was said." There's no point lying about it. "But I would never want to hurt you! And, you know, I ... You know, we ..." I search for the right words, but they're so far out of my reach they could be angels. You know how you flirt with me, but you never take action? You know how I like you a heap, but my best friend is dating your best friend, and I hate him? You know how you're about to tour the country with the world's most famous band and I am always going to live in Lakes? You know, how you're this awesome guy who has never seriously been into me, and I'm some stupid blonde who needs to get the morning-after pill?

Because that's probably the main thing it's gonna boil down to.

He is everything.

I'm nothing.

And despite that moment we shared this morning, the first real thing I've felt from him since we met, we will never, ever work.

"It's fine." Michael throws an arm around my shoulder, pulling my body tight to his in the way *friends* do. It says everything and nothing all at once, and I want *this*. I want him, me together.

It sucks that it will never work out.

We start walking toward the counter, and I pray that he'll go in front of me so I can discreetly reveal my purchase to the cashier.

"We're good. What's one night between friends?" He smiles and gives my bicep a squeeze, and I genuinely think he means it. Either I've convinced him of my lie, or he doesn't care enough not to play along.

Either way, it's a win.

Michael drops his hold on me and pays for his sun block. He gives the woman behind the counter money to protect him from skin cancer.

He leaves the store, but I see him waiting outside for me. Because he's a good person. Unlike me.

I walk up to the counter as Michael did only seconds

before. Only I give the lady money to protect me from having a baby.

Since I'm having the world's greatest day already, I decide to stop at the sexual health clinic on my way home. Because, you know, why not add embarrassment at the hands of a medical industry professional to my already rapidly growing list of below-average things about today?

I sit in the waiting room for what feels like hours, racking my brain, trying to work out what Michael told me last night, and, oh yeah, *who the hell that guy was.*

"Shouldn't be much longer," the receptionist sticks her head over the counter to reassure me. I give a wan smile. She's said that three times already, the last occasion being forty minutes ago.

My phone buzzes and I fish it out of my pocket, bringing it up in front of me. A lady to my right gives me a disapproving eyebrow raise, as if the vibration from my phone had interrupted her silent musings. *Cow.*

Kate: Happy birthday, hon! Hope you're having an awesome day with considerably less shots than you drank last night. Can't wait to celebrate your being of legal drinking age again later in the week. xoxo

I smile and type out a quick text of thanks, then check my messages again. There are a heap of tags on social media, birthday shout-outs from all my school friends and even one from my cousin, June. Still nothing from Mum or Dad. *Odd.*

"… and if I do that, the burning will stop?" A short, grey-haired man hobbles his way down the hall, leaning on his walker for support. Behind him, a tall bespectacled doctor nods, and says, "That's correct."

"Jeanie will be pleased to hear that!" The old man chuckles, and I smile. This doctor hears embarrassing sexy stuff all the time. At least my problem doesn't involve any strange itching or burning.

"Miss Allison, come through." The doctor gestures down the hallway behind him and I scramble to my feet, walking toward the open door at the end of the hallway.

Once inside the small room I sit down. The walls are a stark white, with a row of Perspex holders containing brochures on all different topics lining the room. I catch a glimpse of *What An Itch Can Really Mean* before I snap my head forward and stare at the doctor, who is now sitting down in front of me. *Focus, Stacey.*

"Now, Miss Allison, what can I do for you today?" The doctor removes his glasses and rubs at his eyes. I glance at the clock, ticking away on the wall. It's three p.m.; he's no doubt exhausted.

"I had potentially unprotected sexual intercourse and wish to be checked for STDs." I hold my head up high. No nervous stuttering this time.

The doctor swallows. "Potentially unpro—"

"Why is everyone so hung up on the potential? I can't remember, but I really don't want any …" I swing my gaze back to the brochures on the wall. "… unpleasant *itches*, or diseases, or warts—oh my God, if I ever …" I shudder. Growing up the youngest in a family of seven has meant a lifetime of hearing dating-gone-wrong stories from my three older brothers and one older sister.

"Okay, so we'll need to do a pap smear. Have you ever had one before?"

I shake my head, no.

"Great. I just need you to lie down on the bed over there, having removed the bottom half of your clothing, please." The doctor turns his back to me and begins shuffling through papers on his desk. "There's a robe you can use to cover yourself."

"All—"

"Underwear included, yes."

I shrug. I know it's a stupid question, but I figured it was worth asking anyhow. Just in case I could be less naked.

I wriggle out of my shorts and underwear, tossing them on the floor underneath the bed. I then gingerly climb up and lie down, the plastic cover making a squelching sound underneath my sweaty skin. I stare up at the roof above me, the ceiling fan spinning lazy circles.

"Ready," I sing out, hands clasped over my ribs.

"Good. I—"

I turn to look at the doctor. He swallows. "The robe, Miss." He promptly turns back around to look at the wall.

I throw my head back. Of course. The robe. This doctor must be seriously doubting my ability to keep my clothes on.

I grab the green terry-towelling number and slide it under me, then wrap it around under my armpits, velcroing it shut.

"Are you done?" the doctor asks.

"Sure am."

"Okay." He walks toward me, plastic gloves covering his hands. He lifts up the robe—what is the big deal about, anyway, if he's just going to go lifting it?—and grabs an instrument that looks disturbingly like a pair of tongs had sex with a pair of scissors, resulting in this odd monstrosity. I suck in a breath. He's not going to …

"This may feel a little uncomfortable …"

Ouch! Yep, he's going to. I cringe. Uncomfortable, my ass. This feels like someone is stretching my private bits and then—ugh! Scraping something …

I clench my eyes shut tight, my teeth grinding together. If I make it out of this room alive, I will travel to every single high school in the area and preach the number one reason why you shouldn't have unprotected sex. This cruel and unusual punishment is worse than listening to nails scraping down a chalkboard.

Actually? That. That's exactly what this feels like.

"Just try to relax," the doctor says, and it strikes me once more the injustice of it all. Here he is, sticking some horrible duck bill-shaped monstrosity in my lady bits, and I don't even remember his name. Still, I don't think he'd appreciate my 'some guys take you to dinner and a movie' joke, so I remain silent.

Finally, after what feels like ten minutes, the doctor tells me to shut my legs—no doubt a message he's hoping I take home with me—and get dressed again. Five minutes later and I'm sitting back at the desk while he gathers a few more notes.

"And how many sexual partners have you had?" Doctor— quick check of his nametag—Higgins pushes his glasses back up his nose. I shift in my seat. Ugh. Did questions get any more embarrassing than this?

"Are you after a specific timeframe?" I wrinkle up my nose. *It's worth a shot ...*

"Since you were first sexually active ..." He consults his notes from earlier in my visit. That was before the ultimate insult the medical health profession paid to females, the *I'm going to stick some claws inside you, stretch you and scrape you*, also known as the pap smear. "... two years ago."

"Three," I mumble. Okay, so I'm not exactly a shrinking violet when it comes to the sexual relations department, but I'm certainly not a whore-bag, like some of the other chicks in school. And they were all when I was of legal age. Hell, compared to Boobs Becky, I'm basically Mother Teresa.

Dr Higgins sighs and scratches his balding head, then clasps his hands between his knees and leans forward to look at me, to really eyeball me in the way only disapproving adults can. My stomach once again tries to heave its way out of my throat, and I decide to only take the one pill at a time. I'm hungover enough as it is—surely adding nausea to the mix is a bad idea.

"You know, that's quite a few for a person of your age." The doctor raises his eyebrows. "It's important to remember that sex is important, not just something you should be giving away at the drop of a hat. The rate of teen pregnancy in this area is—"

"I know, I know. And I'll never do it again. I already got the morning-after pill from the pharmacist." I nod.

Shame washes over my body again and I tilt my head back to stare at the ceiling. *Why, oh why, had I had that seventh shot?*

"I'll have your results for the STD tests back within the week. Call me between two and half past next Wednesday, and I'll let you know if anything shows up." Dr Higgins hands me a piece of paper his printer spat out with his name and phone number on it.

"Thanks." I take it and stand to leave, grabbing my purse from the arm of the seat as I do so.

I make my way to the door and turn the handle.

"And Stacey?" Dr Higgins asks.

I spin around. "Yes, Doctor?"

"Be more careful next time."

I get home and pop pill number one in the car, dry-swallowing it and hating the feel as it forces its way down my throat. I put the cardboard box just under the seat to avoid any prying family eyes, making a mental note to come back for round two later. It won't be safe from my nosy family inside.

"Hey, Mum," I say as I walk into the kitchen. Immediately, the seductive aromas of vanilla and dark chocolate fight for my attention. *Mmm …*

"Hi, dear." Mum gives me a brief glance then continues stirring something on the stove. She dips a plump finger in and sucks it into her mouth, a satisfied smile appearing a second later. She gives a brisk nod and puts down her spoon.

"Whatcha making?" I ask, eying the mixture. It's blond, with dots of chocolate-brown littered through it. *Choc-chip? Please not fruit cake …*

"Nothing, dear." Mum dusts her hands off on her apron.

"Not a … birthday cake?" I smile, knowing that's exactly what it is. Every year, Mum makes us cakes. *Every year …*

But the words are like bullets. Mum freezes in her tracks, her hands thrown in the air like mini grenades. "I forgot," she says through gritted teeth.

She forgot? My eighteenth birthday, and she forgot? What could possibly be so important that she didn't remember my—

"I'm so sorry, possum. It's just that everything has been so busy these last few weeks, with work, and your sister's promotion, and Steve's marriage …"

My jaw drops. She really didn't remember. But … it's my *birthday,* my eighteenth, the one that's supposed to mark my coming into adulthood. How did it just slip her mind? She's my mother, for crying out loud.

I open and shut my mouth like I'm a goldfish. I don't know what to say. Surely every parent is supposed to remember the anniversary of the day they gave birth! It would have been one helluva painful day; at the very least she should remember and celebrate that she's not in labour anymore.

Then I look at her, and the apology on her face, printed in her eyes … it freaking sucks, but I can't be angry with her. What's it going to do? What will it achieve?

I make a silent vow to myself. *When I become a mum, I'm going to celebrate every milestone of my child's life. Every. Single. One.*

The thought gives me comfort. Enough to school my features before Mum accuses me of being a brat.

She walks forward and throws her arms around me. She smells of cinnamon, and small flour dust clouds tornado up in the air around us.

"We will get you a present." Mum presses a quick kiss to the top of my forehead. "Now go clean your room. You know Shae wanted tonight to be special."

Shae. How could I forget? The world's most amazing sister, no doubt adding some routine to her act tonight, such as *completing her law degree as the youngest student in Australia* or *becoming the only female partner in the best law firm in the city.*

"I think she's closer to buying a house," Mum squeaks. "She might be moving out."

I smile. I love Shae, I really do, and knowing she is happy is freaking awesome.

No, really.

It is.

Even if it hurts, just a little.

"We can make this a joint cake," Mum says, spooning the mixture into a baking dish. "A Happy House-Buying Shae and Happy Birthday Stacey cake. Has a ring to it, doesn't it?"

I nod. "Sure does."

Mum doesn't respond, so I turn and walk upstairs. My feet feel like lead as they drag over the carpet. I reach my room and grab some clean clothes from my pink dresser—a hangover from when I was five—then walk into the bathroom. I need another shower.

Swish.

Water steams out of the showerhead and I scald myself underneath it. I grab the loofah and start scrubbing, scrubbing till my skin feels almost raw. I want to be clean. I want to be so damn clean I am shiny.

Slut.

I scrape particularly hard over my nether regions, the harsh material rubbing my nipples till the skin breaks and red specks of blood rise to the surface.

Then, when I can clean no more, I turn the taps to closed. The water doesn't stop running, though. It keeps leaking from my eyes.

After I'm dry, I drag myself to bed. I'm so exhausted. I feel it in my limbs, my eyes, and my brain. Everything is slow, sluggish, and foggy. I just want to sleep now, for a very long time. My eyes are closed before my head rests upon my pillow.

Happy birthday to me.

week two

November 26

"YOU GUYS! Can you please get into alphabetical order?" I stamp my foot from my position at the top of the stairs. My hair swishes from side to side. Graduation is about to start in two minutes time, and not only are people not ready, my mother is here.

Yes. You heard it here first.

For the first time in my entire schooling career, my mum has graced an awards ceremony.

I scan the area one more time, just as the door to the room opens. Dave and Kate slink in, hands wrapped around each other. It's like watching a porno, the way he gropes her in public. I shudder. He's someone I'll be glad to lose track of once school finishes. I see him with Kate—the way he talks her down, making her feel like an accessory, not her own awesome self. I grit my teeth. *Jerk.*

"Oh, Kate. Good, you're here." I bounce over to Kate's side, scanning her up and down. "I was getting worried. What took you so long?"

"You know … she couldn't decide what to wear." Dave

jokes. Only, I can't see him. My eyes are fixed on Michael, who is walking up behind him. Michael, who is looking anywhere but at me right now.

"But … it's school uniform today." Even as I say the words, I realise how stupid I sound. I tilt my head to the side. My mind is a million miles from here and smack bang in Michael town. *Is this the last time I'll see him?*

No, you idiot. He's in a band, and you have tickets to their gig next week. I pat my subconscious on the back. Good thinking, brain. We just bought ourselves an extra week of hang-time.

"Well helloooo, Stacey." The guy I'm trying not to stare so obviously at joins our group, giving the back of my skirt a quick tug. I scowl and quickly smooth it down. Heat flushes my cheeks. Was that skirt-tug a subtle reminder about keeping my assets covered in the future?

Michael claps his hand on Dave's shoulder. "Dave, man, how you doing?"

"I think I'll be better in an hour or so."

"I know what you mean."

Michael looks across the group to me. I look at him, and I'm trapped in those stupid chocolaty eyes with their little flecks of irritating hazel and putrid gold flicked through them. *God*, could he be more annoying?

"Not to interrupt your male bonding session, but can you please line up alphabetically? It's im*por*tant." I clasp my hands in front of me and conduct what I hope is a feminine eyelash batting, and not a crazy-person-with-something-in-their-eye move.

"Your wish is my command." Michael bows.

I blink. So … we really are good? And we are friends? Friends who probably won't hang out once school is over, though. After all, it's not like he's ever asked for my number, and he is in a band, and—

Hush. This is a problem I don't have time to sort the answer to right now.

"Right." I narrow my eyes at him, then spin on my heel. "I'll see you when we're graduates, Kate." I throw one hand up in the air and charge to the front of the line.

Thu-thunk, thu-thunk, thu-thunk.

Why the hell is my heart pounding so fast?

Just breathe, Stacey. Breathe.

"We're ready," Miss Lucas, the assistant principal, sticks her head through the doorjamb. "I don't suppose you could …?" She jerks her head toward the students behind me, and I nod and smooth down my skirt.

"Shame we can't offer you any extra credit for that," Miss Lucas says, but I don't miss the way her eyebrows jump up and down. I shake it off. I'm used to my teachers thinking I'm an idiot. When at fourteen you get caught making out with a guy behind the hall instead of participating in school sport, you're generally not referred to as a promising student.

But the past is the past. It's time to graduate the hell out of this thing.

I turn to face the masses. "Everybody, please line up now," I say. People keep talking, too excitedly involved in catching up on the weekend's gossip—for the last time ever, mind you. Our final day of school. I swallow. "They have started already."

In what feels like two seconds, I hear my name being called and I step forward and out in front of the audience.

"Please, a reminder to hold your applause till the end," Mr McDonald, our principal, says as I scan the crowd, looking for my family. He needn't have bothered. When I finally see Mum in the audience, she's texting, or scrolling through some social media feed on her phone. I force a smile for the photographer. At least her phone's on silent.

A *ding* echoes throughout the auditorium. Mum shoves her phone in between her legs and focuses her attention on stage as the parents around turn to look at her.

Or, I thought it was on silent.

I look at my feet.

Time snaps back in and I walk to my spot with the two students whose surnames come before my own, holding my graduation certificate in front of my chest, just how I'm supposed to. I watch as student after student takes the stage, some to beaming smiles of parents in the front row, others to a disinterested eyebrow or two.

Michael walks out to collect his certificate, and his mother stands—actually stands—to cheer him on (silently, of course) and take a picture. His cheeks flush red, and then he looks over at me. I smile. He winks.

A pang of something strikes me in the heart, and I push it away. It's Michael. He is leaving. I am … staying. Insert a round of applause for me here.

More of my friends and some people I barely know walk out and take their certificates, lining in rows behind me and the other ten students whose surnames begin with the letter *A*. Michael is behind me. His breath is warm on my neck. I can't help swaying backwards.

And then *it* happens.

"Kate Tomlinson," Mr McDonald says. Kate walks across the stage, her cheeks flushed red. She never likes being the centre of attention; God knows why. She's beautiful, funny, smart, and dating a guy who is going to take her traveling across the country as his tour manager.

She shakes our principal's hand, then moves over in front of the photographer for the money shot. I hear the guy, some dweeby year ten student, clear his throat, then announce, "Okay, taking your photo in three, two—"

"Yyyyyyes! That's my daughter!"

The slurred voice comes from the very back of the auditorium, accompanied by over-enthusiastic applause.

What.

The.

Hell?

"Good job, Katie! Good—yob." I crane my neck to the back of the hall, and that's when I see him. Kate's dad, Paul, who left her and her mum a little more than a year ago with no apparent reason.

Now he's shown up at graduation … *drunk?*

"Uh, I must remind you that you need to, uh, hold your applause to the end." Mr McDonald pushes his thick, tortoiseshell-framed glasses back up his nose as he attempts to take control of the situation.

"My! My girl!" Paul claps harder, his face red and his eyes fixated on my best friend, who is apparently frozen into place. The parents in the audience watch the scene unfold as if it's a game of tennis. Kate's dad. Kate. Kate's dad. Kate.

"Yaaaaaaaaaaay Katie!"

This time, one of the teachers walks over to him, no doubt asking him to shut the hell up. I look over at Kate. Her face is white, her lips a thin line, her eyes empty pools. It's at that moment that the dweeby photographer decides to do his freaking job and snap her picture. I shake my head. *Idiot.*

"Miss Tomlinson, we'll ask you to move along now." Miss Lucas, the deputy, puts a gentle hand in the small of Kate's back and steers her to join the rest of us on the floor.

At the back of the room, Kate's mum, Deborah, has reached Paul's side, and has her hand out as if to comfort him. He flinches away with a wild lash of his arm, then starts a weird drunken ramble, the word "Kate" and "baby" the only coherent terms among it.

A rumble of low voices washes over the audience, and I push my way through the other students to Kate, who is standing in the back row, her arms trembling.

"Kate, what's going on with your dad?" I go to rub her shoulder, but fold my arms under my chest instead, pressing my lips together. She looks like one warm gesture could bring her apart. I can't be the one to do that.

"I don't know." The words are so soft; I lean in to hear them better.

"I've gotta get back to my place up front, but we'll talk about this later, yeah?"

Kate nods and I move back to my spot. Mr McDonald clears his throat, "ahem"ing into the microphone over and over again.

It's pointless. Everyone watches, their hushed voices still continuing as two teachers escort Paul out of the hall, both with an arm around his.

Everything goes back to normal, and the rest of the ceremony plays out. Well, as normally as it can, given the circumstances.

There are times in your life when seconds seem to drag out for hours. Graduation is like that. Particularly the last few minutes.

Miss Lucas announces the heads of each subject. I shift my weight from foot to foot, trying to avoid pins and needles.

"Head of English … Alexa Chan," Miss Lucas says. We all clap again as Alexa pushes her way from the back of the crowd to the front, a big smile on her face. I clap like I mean it, but my heart and mind are both on Kate.

I scan the crowd once more for Mum. Her phone is back out, and she's texting again. *Maybe she's writing a post on Facebook about how proud she is of me.*

The thought is laughable.

"Head of Drama … Stacey Allison."

I keep staring at Mum, texting on her phone. Someone nudges me in the back. Then someone else.

It's only then I register that the name Miss Lucas has called belongs to me. I shake myself out of my stupor, and can't stop the grin that takes over my face. *Sometimes you get so good at pretending to be someone you're not, you forget to respond when it's the real you.*

I walk up to the stage, shake the principal's hand, and collect my certificate. My knees do this ridiculous wobbling thing, and I smile. Sure, it was only a class of ten, but I came first! At a school subject! I'm freaking out—I'm head of goddamn drama!

This is something I'm good at.

Pretending.

Is it really any wonder?

When the last of the subject toppers are announced, we're all allowed to head back to our seats. I take one last look at the crowd, hoping to finally catch Mum's eye.

Only, she's not there anymore.

I wonder if she really ever was.

I push through the crowd, heading back to my spot in the A row.

Michael winks at me. *Nice work*, he mouths.

"He said, 'Nice ass.'" Dave shakes his head and corrects him.

"Probably because my ass is great." I flash them both a confident smile and turn my head, feeling my hair flick behind me.

My stupid heart, though? It does this dumb stage dive past my ribs, through to my stomach. But no one is there to catch it.

No one's ever there.

It's no wonder I got number one in drama.

I'm really good at pretending.

After the ceremony I push through the crowd, trying to get to the back to find Kate, but it's too late. When I finally reach her, Dave's mother is embracing her. That woman smells like a perfume parlour and acts like she's drunk a bottle.

"We are all so worried about poor Deborah—I mean your mother, dear." Mrs Belmonte sighs as she pulls Kate into her ginormous boobs and squishes a little. Her voice is loud enough for everyone outside the hall to hear it. Hell, I'd be surprised if people down the road at the supermarket didn't catch that remark.

I make a mental note to text Kate later instead. Looks like she's tied up.

I scan the crowd, looking for the familiar blonde that screams *mother* to me, but she is nowhere to be found. I fish my phone out of my pocket to text her, but see she's beaten me to it.

Mum: Had 2 go. Love U

I take a deep breath. You know what? At least she came. She came to my graduation. Can I really be upset that she left early?

"So, your latest conquest spells like a twelve-year-old girl."

I spin around to see Michael, standing way too close to me in this sea of people. He is fixed board-straight, hands in his pockets, brows arched. Smug bastard.

"Cut the crap, Michael." I roll my eyes and give his stomach a tiny punch. *Ow.* Seriously, how the hell did he get abs? "Congratulations on graduating, and all that."

I turn and start to walk toward the parking lot.

"The conversation isn't over." His voice is stern, not joking like he had been before the ceremony. His feet crunch the gravel behind me.

"It takes two to tango."

"Then let's dance, baby." He steps around in front of me so I almost run smack-bang into his chest. It is eye-level with me, and I swallow. My gaze travels over his pecs, his shoulders, his freaking Adam's apple …

Pull yourself together, bitch!

"Last time I saw you, we were friends. The time before, you basically called me a tramp. Now you're accusing me of having some dumbass boyfriend? I don't know where you get your information from, but I'm not seeing anybody. Snap out of it."

"So who's sending you texts full of grammatical errors that say they love you?"

I frown. What is he—

Oh God. Seriously?

"My mother, you idiot." I step around him and keep walking.

Feet shuffle in the gravel and soon he's by my side again. "Your mum texts like that?" He screws up his nose, his pace easily matching mine. Hell, the man has beanpoles for legs. Jack could climb those things and find a giant at the top, and—

Heat flushes my cheeks again as the image of a potential giant organ at the top of Michael's legs forms in my brain. Since when did I become so sex-obsessed?

"Why didn't she stay till the end?" he presses, and all

thoughts of his potential appendage fly from my brain. I'm used to people picking on me, but people don't insult my family. It's just not what they do.

"Shae's buying a house and moving out of home, and getting married, and has a promotion at work. Steve is moving out of home and who knows what promotion Sean has now. Scott is off saving the world somewhere still, and Mum doesn't have time to text in complete words, but it doesn't mean she doesn't understand them."

To prove my point, I bring my phone up to my face and type a few quick words.

Me: Thanks again for coming. Meant a lot to me.

"So, what are you doing?"

"Hmm?" I stop walking when we reach my car. It's a hand-me-down from Shae, of course, but I know I'm lucky. Hell, not everyone my age has wheels.

"What are you doing? Your sister and brothers are ruling the world ... what are you planning on doing?" Michael leans up against the door of my Corolla.

"Graduating?" I shrug. "Trying to get boys who follow me to stop blocking the entrance to my car?"

"I mean, next year." Michael gives this easy smile. It's not enough to calm the panic in my body, though. I hate this question; I hate it with a passion. Especially from *him*.

"I don't know." I shrug. "It's the year of Stacey; I'm going to live it up."

He shakes his head. "You must be doing something aside from partying. Kate's going on tour with us—you're not jetting off for a gap year? Or working somewhere glamorous?"

He means well. I can hear it in his tone, see it in his smile. Something in those small things breaks me, cracks me open just enough to let seven tiny words spring free from my mouth. "I just haven't sorted it out yet."

I must sound as pathetic as I think I do, as suddenly

Michael's hand is on my shoulder, his large chest right in front of me again.

"Hey." He gives the top of my arm a rough stroke. "You're not supposed to have it all sorted."

"Yeah, well, everyone else kinda does, right?" I shrug his hand off. Even though I want nothing more than to let his comfort soak in.

"Yeah, but you know … you don't have to want to do anything."

"It's not that I don't want to do anything—it's that I kind of want to do everything."

"Of course you do." Michael laughs, his face breaking into a smile, and I instantly feel some relief. Relief about what, I don't know. That he doesn't think I'm a drop kick? "Remember that time in tenth grade when you took on every elective possible?"

"I forgot about that." I giggle along with him. "Who volunteers to do sixteen units when you only have to do ten?" I silently add *and then fails six of them*. I was always good at dreaming; at making plans I couldn't necessarily follow through.

"But that's just you, Stace. Hell, even two weeks ago. We were only doing one round of shots, then you had, like, seven …" As he says the words, something flashes over his features. He's not smiling anymore. He drops his hand.

My phone vibrates and I check the message.

> **Mum: U don't need 2 thank me. Not like I have 2 go 2 ur college grad. Lol.**

Silence.

I blink. Look again. But the message is still there.

It shouldn't surprise me. Hell, my own parents sometimes make "dumb blonde" jokes about me. But knowing hurt is coming, knowing that there's likely to be pain, doesn't make you prepared for it.

It doesn't numb the sting.

Michael's jaw drops so low, I can practically see his tonsils. I shove my phone in my pocket, desperate to hide the offending item from his view.

"That's not very supporti—"

"Just leave it." I put up one hand, using it as a barrier between Michael and myself.

"I didn't mean to offend you," he says. Those damn eyes are boring into my soul again. How'd he get so good at that? "It's just that it seems kind of an odd thing for a mother to say."

"She's joking. She wrote *LOL*."

"She probably thinks it means Lots Of Love."

This time, I give him a look that I hope is somewhere between the Wicked Witch of the East and Cruella de Vil in intensity. "Can I please hop in my car now?"

Michael steps forward, and just as I think he's finally doing something nice as I asked, he grabs my cell from my pocket and starts rapidly typing into it.

"Give it back." I lunge for it, but it's no use. The guy is practically a giant. *With beanstalk legs and a large fictional package ...*

"Please?" I jump up to try and wrench it from his hands, but all he has to do is subtly shift from his left foot to his right one to keep me from reaching my goal. I grab onto his arm and pull, trying not to notice how good he smells—like pine and soap and man—and wondering if he's always smelt like that.

"Here." He hands it back to me.

"What'd you say?" I scroll to the messages section of my phone, but the conversation with Mum isn't there. "Where ... did you delete that conversation?"

"Joke or not, you don't need something toxic like that in your life." He's all serious again. "You shouldn't let people drag you down, Stacey."

"Just one more reason why I need you to step away from my car." I try to lighten the mood. Neither of us is laughing.

"I put my number in your phone"—Michael folds his arms across his chest— "not that I expect you'll need it. But in case you ever can't get in touch with Kate while we're on tour. Or if you need a birthday bacon and egg roll, or something."

Or if I need a guy to give me a lift home after I have sex with some stranger I can't remember.

"Thanks." I pull open my car door and slide into the seat, the engine turning over easily once I start her up. I am fairly sure I'll delete the number as soon as I get home. I can't have Michael. He's more than I deserve.

I wind down my window and wave to him. "It's been nice knowing ya." I wink. I know I'll see him again. Hell, he's in a band with my best friend's boyfriend. I have tickets to their show next Wednesday. I'll be lucky to avoid him.

I accelerate and slowly move away when he raises his hand in the universal *stop* gesture. I slam on the brakes, even though I'm not really going fast enough to justify it.

Michael does a slow jog and halts at my window, resting his hands on the door.

"For the record, I know however many things you do, you're gonna be great at 'em."

"Things?" I blink.

"Anything. Everything." He smiles, and the grin says it all. No matter what career I choose, Michael thinks I can do it. "All the things."

Warmth floods me, from head to toe. *But they're only words …* My subconscious is a doubting bitch, apparently.

I smile and dip my head. "Thanks."

"No worries." He takes a step back and pats the roof of my car, sending me on my way. I accelerate once more, but I don't miss his parting words as I pull out of the lot.

"Who names five kids all starting with the same letter, anyway?"

I keep driving.

"And congrats on the drama score!"

When I get home, I go through my car, taking wadded up notes from class and walking them into the garage to throw them in the bin.

It's dark in the garage, and the smell of metal with a hint of garden permeates the air. I lift open the garbage lid to throw my never-to-be-needed-again notes in, and that's when I see it, sitting on the top shelf beside a giant box marked *Christmas Decorations*. A small metal tin, covered in black marker, my name scrawled in shaky print on the front.

Memories flash through my mind. Camping down the south coast. Chasing Thunder, our old pet dog. Playing dolls with Shae.

I pull the box down, then wipe the thick layer of dust from my hands on my school skirt. *Not like I need to keep it clean anymore.*

I know exactly what's inside. The letters our teacher, Mrs Harris, made our twelve-year-old selves write to our eighteen-year-old ones. I smile, remembering the big deal Mum and Dad had made of me then. Back when everything was easy and simple, when Dad wanted to keep this memory trapped in a box. I wonder if they even knew we still had it.

The box creaks as I open it, and I pull the yellowed paper out. It smells like crayon, and something else—age, perhaps. I step outside, leaning up against the car to read my words, a smile playing on my lips.

Dear Eighteen-Year-Old Stacey,

Hi! You're such a grown-up now. I hope you've gotten a heap taller, 'cause if not, you're never going to be able to reach the biscuits Mum keeps on the top shelf of the pantry, and that'd suck.
I also hope you've gotten boobs like Shae's. She has good boobs. All the boys say so. More than that, I hope you and Shae are still best friends and that you hang out all the time. You won't make up worlds

anymore, or play tip, but maybe you'll do grown-up things together—go to the movies, or visit cafes and stuff.

You'll be finished high school, and about to go to uni, like Scott, and maybe you can be a lawyer or something. Something that will let you buy whatever house you want, so you can stay close to Shae and Sean and Scott and Steve. Or, maybe you could just buy a really big house so we can all live together, but so that Shae and you don't have to share a room anymore. Then you could have sleepovers.

I don't think you'll be married, but you'll have a boyfriend. He'll be handsome and he'll kiss you and your knees will feel weak, like Shae says hers do when Danny kisses her. You won't fall over, though.

I can't wait to be Eighteen-Year-Old Stacey!

Love,

Twelve-Year-Old Stacey

My heart is lead. It *tick-tock*s like a pendulum inside my chest, a heavy weight pulsing inside me. I bite down on my lip to stop the stupid tears from falling.

I'm not going to university. I doubt I'll ever earn enough money to buy a house, let alone one big enough for the whole family—but why would I want to? Shae barely speaks to me, and the rest of them I only see on special occasions. I sure as hell don't have a boyfriend—in fact, the guy I've like had a girlfriend, and then got a gig touring the country. Plus, he's everything good.

I am nothing but trouble.

I crumple the letter up and open my car door, shoving it in my glove box. That one piece of paper is hurting me so much, and yet I can't bring myself to throw it away. It's a reminder that once I thought I could be something. *Do* something.

I grab my bag from the floor of the car, and that's when I see I see it: a small cardboard box sitting on the floor.

"Shit," I curse and snatch it up. With shaking hands I lift the lid. A quick tilt south and the silver foil packet comes flying out. On one side, there's a popped hole where a pill once had been.

On the other, there's one very-much-still-intact, not-consumed pill.

The one that in my sleep-deprived state, I clearly forgot to take.

Double shit.

week THree

November 30

FEEL LIKE I'm in *Groundhog Day*. Only, it's more like Groundhog Minute. And it goes a little something like this:

Check watch.

Wonder where Kate is.

Listen to girl in cubicle one vomit her guts up.

Be thankful that the Coal concert is in the venue next door, so after the time is up I won't have to visit these toilets and possibly get vomit on my new—*hot*—shoes again.

Check watch.

Sip beer.

Repeat.

Okay, so I may be exaggerating a little. It has only been five minutes of waiting, but when you're leaning up against a white tiled wall in a small-as-a-freaking-snail-shell toilet cubicle, waiting for the little stick you've peed on to change colour, five minutes sure feels like a long time.

I put my beer down on the toilet seat, and check my watch again. It has been five-point six minutes since I'd managed to perform what I am now referring to as a great feat of skill and athleticism—peeing into the world's smallest cup so I could stick a piece of white plastic into it.

The minimum wait time was three minutes, but I hated the thought of checking and reading it wrong, or checking and it not being fully developed, so I've left the gross little cup on the floor until now.

But now, five minutes in, almost double the time the box said the little genies inside the stick need to work their pregnancy-foresight magic, I have no more excuses.

It is time.

I take another swig of my beer, and place the empty bottle in the tiny toilet bin. Sure, it may not have been the most hygienic place to have an early-evening beverage, but given my current state of nerves and the freak out I'd experienced since I found that stupid pill on the floor of my car, it seemed relevant. I was late. Not the good, fashionable kind—no, this was a *late* of the maybe-a-sperm-and-my-egg-got-it-on variety. It was only frustrating I hadn't found the time alone in my multi-sibling household to test this out sooner.

I bend down and grab the top of the plastic stick from the cup. I give it a few tiny shakes, because *ew, pee*, and then hold it up in front of my face, my eyes scrunched shut.

I take a deep breath in, sucking it right to the bottom of my lungs, and let it go through pursed lips. *I can do this. I can freaking* do *this. I can—*

"Stacey? You in there?"

My heart leaps into my throat and I slam my body back against the door, as if she knows exactly what cubicle I'm in, exactly where to find me, and exactly what it is I'm doing. *Just keep breathing …*

"Stace? Babe?"

I tilt my head back and let it slap against the wooden door behind me.

"I saw you walk in, and you've, um … been here a while, and I wanted to know if you need me to get you a water or anything." Kate pauses, and I swallow. "Or, like, some gastro meds?"

I drop the stick and spin around, flinging the door open and charging out into the basin area of the ladies room.

"I do *not* have gastro!" I say, my hands flying around me in defiance.

"Sorry, I just thought that maybe, you—"

"Just because a girl spends five minutes and"—quick watch check—"fifty-six seconds in the bathroom, she has to be having a diarrhoea episode?"

"No!" Kate's hands fly in front of her face. "I wasn't saying it had to be that, I just—"

A girl walks past her, her eyebrows nearing her hairline as she purses her lips. She is not impressed. She walks into cubicle three.

"Hmm?" I fold my arms across my chest.

"I just wanted to make sure you're okay." Kate looks up at me with those blue pools of emotion from under her thick, dark lashes, and smiles. "And I was worried you had gastro."

I slowly nod. More guilt washes over me. She's had an embarrassing father incident recently, and is planning on losing her V-card tonight. I'm screaming at her for trying to get me some medication.

My mind runs through the options:

Tell her you're a sleazy ho and slept with a guy you don't remember, and so you're doing a pregnancy test.

Admit that you have gastro, endure severe teasing, but come out of it skank-scent-free.

Say you're in there for a friend she doesn't know ... *and seriously hope the girl in cubicle one is over her gastro-vomiting stint and that you don't have to follow through in a support role.*

"Well, I'm fine." I nod. Denial it is. Seems like the easiest route to take. "Hey, so how are things with your dad?"

Kate runs a hand through her long brown hair and it falls back into place perfectly. Looking closer, I can see the cracks in her façade. The purple bruises under her eyes. The way her lips press together before she speaks.

"It's ... complicated." Kate pauses, looking at herself in the mirror. She grabs a compact out of her handbag and powders her cheeks. "And tonight's the big night on top of all that."

"Eee!" I squeal, grabbing her arms and pulling the puff away from her face. "I'm so freaking excited for you! Are you nervous?"

Red flushes over her face, and I mentally kick myself. Of course she's nervous.

"You are going to be fine." I tuck her hair behind her ear. It's hard to believe that my best friend is a virgin, and I could be a pregnant. *Ew.* To a guy I don't know. *Double ew.*

Kate looks at the floor, pressing the toe of her ballet flat and rubbing it into a spot. "I've just got a lot going on right now."

"I know, hon. I can't even imagine, with this, and your dad drunk, and—" Kate takes in a sharp breath, and I bite my lip. Another girl struts into the bathroom. God, this Coal band really are popular if they're attracting skanks of the fake-boobed, botoxed-lipped proportion. "Look, you're gonna nail it tonight. Just relax, remember to breathe, think sexy thoughts, and hey, maybe go down on him first, so he's lubed as well as you."

"Ew!" Kate groans.

"Excuse me, are you still using that cubicle?" the girl asks, hands on her clearly visible hips.

"Yeah, just a sec." I give Kate one final squeeze as Booby and Lippy makes her move toward my cubicle.

Kate walks out the door and I turn and slam the cubicle door in Booby's face, clicking the lock shut behind me. It's now been at least eight minutes. I can't hide from this anymore.

I bend down to pick up the stick, and a tiny part of me, connected to my heart? It dies.

It dives off a cliff.

It falls through endless space, with no respite in sight, and then it crashes on the craggy rocks below, impaling itself.

I hold the white piece of plastic level with my eyeline. My hand shakes, and I try with everything I have to keep it solid. To keep it steady.

I blink, twice, trying to focus on the little white stick with the thin pink lines on it.

Two lines.

Pregnant.

My knees shake, literally shake, like they do in movies, and I'm no longer looking at a stick. All of a sudden I'm on the cold, tiled floor, one hand in a pile of suspicious wet substance, the other holding the tiny white stick high above my head to prevent contamination.

"I'm fucking pregnant," I whisper.

Everything goes black.

If seven shots of tequila had gotten me into this mess, I didn't see any good reason why it couldn't get me out of it. I needed to forget.

"Tequila, thanks." I hand over a note to the bartender, and he nods, turns away, then slams a glass down in front of me.

I pick it up and walk to the side, then take a sip. The liquid burns as it slides down my throat, thick and acidic, clawing its way down through my insides. Ugh. That tastes horrid.

I look back over at the bar where people line up, pressing for the bartender's attention. I spot the bottle of Patron on the shelf, the no smoking signs, the responsible service of alcohol signs, the—

The sticker. Right next to the bottle of tequila, funnily enough.

Drinking when pregnant can harm your baby.

Frick. *Really, God? You're going to guilt trip me now?*

I have no idea what to do with this stupid not-even-real-yet human, but I don't know that I can murder it. I raise my glass to take another sip, but the stupid sign catches one of the lights and flashes, mocking me, taunting me.

I press my body up against the wall. After a quick look to

either side, I spill the drink on my shirt, then dip my fingers in the glass and pat a little behind my ears for good measure. Yes, I am crazy, but I don't want to drink—because I'm pregnant—but I do want Kate to think I've been drinking—because I don't want her to know.

I wonder if I can get drunk by osmosis? I silently pray for a yes.

Shaking my head, I search for Kate in the crowd. She's right where I left her, her eyes fixed on the stage. God, she's a good girlfriend.

I push my way through the crowd, but it's hot in here. My arms stick to my sides, and my vision blurs in and out. My head pounds, and I clutch my stomach. *I turned down tequila for you, womb spawn! Quit it with the dizzy-making.*

"Are you okay?" Kate puts her hand on my arm. I didn't realise I'd been swaying, but as soon as she steadies me, everything stops moving. Lesson learned.

"I ... fine," I stutter out. She raises her eyebrows, and I ignore her. She's never been one for drinking, and I'm sure she's judging me, but I don't mind. Right now, I'd rather her judge me on booze over babies.

Minutes later, Dave & The Glories come on stage, and Kate lets out an almighty cheer that makes something in my heart snap. Seeing her, so proud of Dave—someone who loves her—someone she's going to travel across the country for ...

I look up on stage for Michael, and there he is: striking his notes on the bass guitar like it's so freaking easy, so second nature to him to make an instrument sound that good. His eyes roam over the audience, floating over all the girls who cheer the name of his band.

And then they land on me.

Me.

Heat rushes through me as I grin, one of those ear-to-ear numbers you see in cheesy romance movies. What had he said to me the night of that party? What if ...

I blink.

I'm pregnant.

I blink again.

Michael looks away.

What the hell am I thinking? He hasn't asked me out before, and he is in a band about to go on tour. Michael and I don't stand a chance. I'm pregnant with some random guy's baby.

I glance at Kate again. She nods her head, mouthing all the words. She's so cute; her eyes are focused on Dave. I can't wait to get some time alone with her, to talk through this whole freaking mess. Hell, maybe I'll even tell her how I really feel about Michael. From the sly comment she made while we lined up to get in, I have a feeling she might suspect anyway.

Halfway through the boys' set, someone hands me a drink, and I knock it back without thought. God, I'm thirsty. And my vision is … vision … *baby.* How my brain gets there I didn't know, but it does, and the feeling is like being knocked over with a lead balloon.

A pair of unfamiliar arms creep around my waist and I shrug them off, only to feel them force their way back again. I look down in irritation and push them away again. *Find one of the million single girls here,* I feel like saying. That is, of course, before I remember I am single.

Even if I have a baby growing inside of me.

I shake my head. Maybe I need to find a random guy. Someone to take my mind off this shit for one night, until I can work out what the hell I am going to do.

Arms from behind me move with my hips, rocking up and down to the beat of the music. It's sexy and slow, and feeling his strong arms around me, his hardness behind me, the sweat of his body against mine … it makes me temporarily forget.

His breath warms my ear, and then he sucks on my neck. I raise my arms and entwine them around his head, trying to lose myself in the feeling and pretend I haven't seen the anger on Michael's face as he strummed that last riff.

Kate gives me a look and moves a little farther into the crowd. *Yep, slutty Stacey is at it again.* I can practically touch her disapproval. It's not like I'm planning on leaving here with him.

Aside from that horrible night after Joe's, I've only slept with two guys, and they'd all been serious boyfriends at the time. Sure, I flirt a lot, but when your best friend looks at you like that?

It hurts.

The sucking on my neck grows intense, painful, even, and I swipe at the guy's shoulder, trying to push him back. My eyes scrunch shut.

Would doing this make the thing less real?

The … *baby?*

I need to talk to Kate.

"Get off me." This time, my shove is forceful as I jolt the guy back. I spin to face him and he shrugs. I can't really blame him. I've let him dirty dance with me for several songs in a row, and now I have a problem with him sucking on my neck?

Glancing back up on stage, I make eye contact with Michael, at the same time as the random guy places his hands on my hips again—gently this time.

I raise my chin in challenge.

Michael raises his eyebrows.

Then he plays his next eight notes with just one finger.

The middle one.

week four

December 9

IT IS our last night at schoolies, the annual congregation of the recently liberated to celebrate their eighteen-year-old I-can-drink, I-can-legally-vote (hah!) freedom on the Gold Coast of Australia. It is pretty much Vegas by the sea, and I'd booked my flight when Kate first whispered she'd be going with the band.

Granted, things are different now.

Now, Dave is a douchebag. Well, even more of one than I already thought he was.

I don't get angry about many things. But you screw with my friends—seriously, you breathe on them in an incorrect fashion—and I will take your balls, bake them in a pizza, and serve it to your closest acquaintances from here till next Sunday.

Add to the mix the fact that on our first day here, Kate told me her father has Huntington's, a horrible disease that affects your nervous system, resulting in death—and that there's a fifty per cent chance she could have it—and you have a recipe for one hell of a week for Kate. It makes my own slight pregnancy problem seem pale in comparison.

"I've never kissed a guy before," some dickwad in our circle on the beach says, and all around the group, girls lift their glasses in the drinking game that could possibly be renamed 'What Have Girls Done We Can Punish Them For.' Because, seriously. *Seriously.*

We hold our shot glasses to our mouths, then tilt back and let the alcohol fling in. As I'd been doing all night, I let the sweet green liquid fill my mouth, do a pretend and overtly obvious swallow, then grab my pink drink bottle, pretending like I was chasing the Midori with some water, when really I am spitting the alcohol out.

Am I planning on keeping the baby?

No freaking idea.

The one thing I do know is that I'd woken up the morning after the boys' gig with a guilt-induced hangover worse than that felt by a nun at a strip show.

All I'd wanted to do was talk to Kate about it all, but after Dave broke up with her, and then she told me the truth about her and her father and the horrible disease that could kill them? Frick. I can't burden her with my stupid problems. It makes me even more determined not to drink. I can't stand the thought of risking some sort of defect in this child, not when Kate is going through what she is going through.

I sneak a glance at her once more from out the corner of my eye. She is rocking slightly as she sits. Clearly, she didn't have the foresight to bring a spitting bottle.

Because she's not pregnant.

The dark purple bruises under her eyes give her away. I know she hasn't been sleeping, and despite what she said to me earlier about how much fun she's having, this has been one of the worst weeks of her life.

"I'm gonna go," Kate says, standing up and stretching her legs. I look into her eyes; they speak of loneliness and heartache as they have ever since graduation. And hell, since she'd confided in me about what a jackass Dave was, and how crazy her situation at home is, I can't freaking blame her.

"I'll come with you." I stretch my arm up to her and she grips it with her hand.

"No, you stay." She tilts her head toward the blond surfer guy at the edge of the circle. I'd noticed him earlier in the night, and made a subtle show of pretending to Kate I was interested. She kept pushing me to go out and "have a little fun" on our last night in Queensland, and when she says it again now, I screw my eyes shut. How do you tell your best friend you're not interested in all that?

After the argument continues, I decide to give in. If it's going to help Kate sleep easier, knowing I'm 'with' someone else, I am damn well keen.

After some back and forth, Kate leaves, and starts the walk to the hotel. I wait till she's gotten to the boardwalk, and then say my goodbyes to the group.

"Why didn't you just go with your friend, then?" an annoying guy with slicked back hair asks. Somehow, I don't think "*because I'm worried about my potentially vulnerable friend, and spitting is for camels and I'm done*" is a viable answer.

"Get stuffed," I say instead.

I follow Kate as she walks along the boardwalk. She wanders aimlessly, her head turning to look at all the signs as she passes them and for the bazillionth time since she's told me the truth about her dad, I just want to go over there and wrap her up in a big cotton wool ball and squeeze her till she feels so suffocated by affection she can't breathe.

Or something like that, with less death, anyway.

I finally follow her onto the street that leads to our hotel when I see her turn down an alley. I stalk closer to it, my heart pounding. Why is she going down here? The hotel is barely a block away. This must be how mothers feel when their child does something wrong.

Shit.

I am going to be a mother.

Pushing the thought to the back of my mind, I slink alongside the buildings till I get closer to the little A-frame chalkboard that marks the entrance to the alley.

"Fortunes read and futures told …" I breathe. I stick my head down the alleyway just in time to see Kate disappear into a shopfront next to an A-frame identical to the one out on the street. A psychic? That isn't like practical, researching, rational Kate.

I decide to creep a little closer. Maybe I can hear what the psychic tells her, be there for my best friend when she comes out.

I take one tentative step then another, walking on tiptoes so as to avoid potential detection.

Suddenly, a hand claps down on my shoulder. My heart leaps into my throat. I suck in a gasp and spin around as quickly as I can.

"What are you doing?" Michael's deep brown eyes dance in front of mine. I slump against the wall behind me, brushing off his hand and resting my head against the warm, hard bricks.

"You scared the crap out of me," I say. I close my eyes. As much as I'm relieved to know it's not some psycho killer, I'm also as confused as a whale on Ayers Rock. What the hell is he doing here?

"Well, that's what you get for stalking people." Michael shoves his hands into his pockets, a mischievous smile playing across his face.

I give a small shove to his chest. His quite firm, non-moving chest.

Wow.

"What are you doing?" I ask, biting on my lip. The pain allows me to focus on something other than how sexy his chest is. Why hadn't I tried touching it before?

"Following you, following Kate?" His lips rise in a half-smile. I shake my head. "Okay, so our gig was up here, remember? And I knew the hotel you guys were staying at, because Dave spent three hours blowing up over how annoyed he was that Kate moved his penthouse to the sister hotel and had it under her name only."

"And you came here to see us?" I ask. God, does my heart always pound this loud?

"Yep." This time, I'm graced with a fully-fledged grin.

Air rushes out of my lungs, and I can't help but smile. "You know, that's kind of stalky."

"Does that make you uncomfortable?" he asks, and I swallow. Michael takes another step closer to me, and I back up until I am flush with the brick wall. Barely an inch separates our bodies, and with each breath in I take, my chest moves closer to his.

"So … um …" I clear my throat. "Did you just, like, walk the streets to try and find us?"

Look straight ahead. Study the collar of his T-shirt.

Do not make eye contact.

I glance up.

Shit!

DO NOT MAKE EYE TO LIP CONTACT.

"Nah, I was just doing a once over, then I was going to call or something." He runs his hand through his hair, shrugging his shoulders as if it were no big deal.

"Look, I also wanted to say I'm sorry about what a douche Dave has been. I know I texted you, but it just wasn't cool, and I thought I should do an in-person apology."

I nod. "While we're on the subject of apologies …" I clear my throat. My mind flashes back to memories of him sticking his finger up at me as he played. "… I should probably apologise to you."

"What for?" Michael asks.

"For, um …" I bite my lip. Damn him for making this harder! "Letting some guy make out with my neck while you watched?"

If you've ever seen a storm out at sea, you'd know exactly what I'm seeing now. Michael's face goes from sunny, to stormy, to torrential, to sunny again, all in the blink of an eye. Or maybe I'm just flattering myself.

Maybe he is simply confused and has no idea what I'm talking about.

"Not even. It's not like we're dating." He shrugs. A whoosh of air fills my lungs, and I'm not sure if it's clouded with relief or sorrow. Are both this heavy? "Besides, it's not like the kiss was a big deal."

"It … wasn't?"

"Nah, 'course not. You can kiss who you wanna kiss, even if it is some random dude at my concert."

Oh.

He doesn't care.

Double oh.

Michael takes a deep breath in then exhales, his lips forming a small pucker. My disappointment must show on my face, because I can see him processing the thoughts, giving small nods of his head as he no doubt decides what to say next. "Stacey, what you do is your choice. Let's be honest: my whole life you've pretty much acted repulsed by me. It's hardly like I stood a chance with you anyhow."

"Stood a chance?" I practically choke on my tongue. "What the hell are you talking about? You've never even asked me out before."

"Boys tease you because they like you?" Michael asks.

"Seriously?" I shove at his chest. "You thought I was pretty, but a bimbo. Someone you couldn't see a future with." He opens his mouth to speak, but I hold up a finger in protest. "Don't lie. I know it's true." *Everyone does.* No smart girl gets preggers at eighteen.

"Hey, take it easy, Einstein. I didn't know you wanted to be recognised for the scholar that you are," Michael says, a smile warming his face again. "No bimbo I've ever met comes first in drama."

My cheeks warm. "It's just a performance thing; anyone can do it." I shrug, and study the tar beneath me. "And with only nine other people in the class …"

"Hey." Michael places his hand under my chin, tilting it up so I look into his eyes. "Not anyone; *you.*"

This time, the heat flushes through my body and I bite down on the smile that creeps its way to the corners of my mouth. "I guess, I—"

Before I can finish my sentence, Michael grabs my hand and pulls me out of the alleyway, back in the direction I came from. He darts into the shallow of a shopfront and jerks me in after him, my body landing flush against his.

"She's coming," he breathes, the warm air from his words caressing my skin.

He is right in front of me, his arms touching my arms, his legs touching my legs … *his chest touching my chest.*

Swallow.

That is infinitely worse.

"Michael …" I blink. This time there is no *don't look at his eyes* or *please don't look at his lips*. I can't stop myself gravitating toward him. My eyes flick down, looking at his pink lips, imagining how soft they'd feel, how much I want to taste him, and—

"She's gone." Michael steps back.

I turn to face the street and see Kate as she disappears around the corner, heading safely into our hotel.

I want to die. What the hell is going on? Does he like me or not?

And why am I hitting on a guy in a sell-out concert support band if I'm pregnant?

Once again, my stupid reality smacks me in the face. "All right. Well, looks like I'll head back." I put on a cheery face. Yep. Cheery. That's how fake it is.

"I'll walk you back." Michael takes a few steps in the hotel's direction.

"Why?" I narrow my eyes.

"Stace." He runs his hands through his hair again, staring up at the sky. "It's no secret I like you, yeah? And I don't want you to get murdered. Or raped. Or—hell, I don't even want you to get cold."

I give a wry smile. It's a warm summer night, and I can feel the damp sheen of perspiration on my forehead. *At night.*

Still, that isn't what I smile about. He likes me. He really thinks he likes me. *Me!*

On the way back to the hotel, my head keeps swirling with thoughts. I have to deal with this. What the hell am I going to do? Michael. He likes me, but he's leaving. The baby. Hell, my career. I haven't applied for any university courses. I'm not stupid enough to fight my fate. I'm destined to work at the supermarket and marry some guy and sprout out his kids. I've most likely failed three of my subjects, and I doubt you can get a scholarship based on *good at cheerleading and bossing around your peers.* I've always known that.

When you're the only blonde in a family of brunettes, and grew up with lines like "By the time Mum and Dad got around to creating you, all the intelligence genes had been dished out," it's hard to think you can be more. What's the point in trying when you know you're going to fail? Sometimes, it's easier to admit defeat. To admit that just as everyone predicted, I've failed.

What if this baby is the one thing I could be good at?

When we get to the lobby, Michael helps me over to the elevator.

"Well, I guess I'll be go—"

"Stay." The word is out of my mouth before I have time to process it. I want, no, I need him to stay, so badly.

"I don't mean to sound like a dick ... but why?" Michael withdraws his arm and the cool air-conditioned air caresses my back.

"I don't know," I whisper. My bottom lip trembles. "I just ... I don't know." Tears well in my eyes and in a heartbeat, Michael's arms wrap around me and I've never felt safer or more secure while feeling such loss and emptiness inside.

What is right? What is the *right thing* in this situation?

The elevator dings open and Michael and I step inside. I click the button for our floor and watched the numbers flick up, the elevator sending a familiar lurch through my stomach as we pick up speed.

"You okay?" Michael cups my chin, and I give a weak nod. He must think I am a psychopath.

We walk to our door and I usher Michael in, pointing him

toward my room.

"Nice place," Michael whispers, taking in the large, white bed and the view that stretches out over Surfers Paradise below. Lights twinkle from the clubs and pubs on the strip, all the way to the freight ships out at sea in the distance. The city has turned it on tonight.

"Thanks."

Michael sits on the edge of the bed and takes off his shoes.

"Shall we … talk?" Michael asks.

I shrug. For once, I am all out of words.

"How are things with your family?"

The words are so soft, I'm almost not sure I hear them. "What—what do you mean?"

"You know." Michael shrugs and presses his body farther up the bed, relaxing against the headboard. "The mum who said she's not confident in your grades. The overachieving siblings."

"They're fine." I swallow.

"Oh, come on. That must be hard shit to live up to." Michael taps my arm.

"Not really." *Lie.*

"How could it not be? Are you gonna be a doctor?" He edges closer till our legs are touching.

"No." My voice is small.

"Did your mum apologise for that text about not graduating uni?" Michael's voice is proportionately louder to my diminishing one. He seems to tower over me.

"No." Quieter than the last.

"Do you have a steady boyfriend who's about to propose?"

Kapow!

Boom!

Boof!

Owee!

I am in a cartoon. No, I don't have a boyfriend who's about to propose. I have a baby whose fate I have to decide on. I have a guy I really like in my hotel room, who has finally said he has a crush on me but is about to go away on tour while I nurse a baby.

Unless … I don't.

I think about Kate. Can I kill a human when a human my best friend loves is being murdered by a disease?

Can I?

"C'mon, Stace, answer me." Michael bounces the bed a little, snapping my attention back to the present. "I can keep your secrets, you know."

That's when I hear it. Kate's bedroom door opening and shutting. The click of the pipes in the bathroom. The thuds of her footsteps as she walks back to bed.

She can't know I have Michael here. She doesn't need reminding of Dave, and she sure as hell doesn't need to know I'm not hooking up with some random dude on the beach when it was something she had been so adamant about.

I whip around to face Michael. "Pretend to have sex with me."

His jaw drops, his brow furrowed. "What?"

"I don't want Kate to think you're here, or that it's some other guy I'm just … talking with." I throw my hands up. "It's complicated, but she needs to think I'm screwing someone. She was really keen on me making out with a random guy, having fun. Okay?"

Michael is silent for a moment, worrying at his lip. "And why can't she think I'm here?"

"It'll remind her of Dave." And I don't know that I can deal with talking about you being here with me. *Not when I keep thinking about your lips.*

"Stacey, do you like me?" His intense brown eyes bore into mine and I'm naked. To my very soul.

"I … you're a good friend." I nod, slowly.

"That's not what I mean, and you know it," he hisses, pushing up the bed until he's right in front of me. His face is all hard lines, his eyes glittering like stones.

"Yes." The word is an ant. It's that tiny.

"So why can't we *do* something about it?" he yells, and I press my shaking finger to his lips. They're soft, and big, and warm, and *hell* do I want him in this moment more than I ever have before.

"You're in a band … you're going on tour," I mumble, quickly jerking my hand back and picking at the threads on my dress. "And again, I don't want to tell Kate about you because of Dave, and …" The words sound lame, even to me.

"That's wrong; you know that, right?" Michael's eyes flash. "You're so freaking embarrassed of me that you won't tell your best friend that we're—what? Friends?"

"Michael …" I press my hand to his arm. What can I say? I want to be with you, but I'm pregnant, and I have a lot to deal with right now? I want to be with you, but I don't think I can kill this baby and you can't give your career a worthwhile shot if you have a girlfriend back home, let alone a pregnant one? "I just … I just want to give her some space to deal with this, and her dad, okay?"

"And in the morning? What then?" His fierce eyes shine into mine, interrogating me.

"I … I don't know."

He shrugs my hand off his arm, turning his shoulders in on himself.

We sit there in silence. I look out the window again. How can the world look so pretty when it's really so damn ugly?

"Do you know how I knew you liked me?" Michael whispers. I shake my head, refusing to make eye contact. "It was one of the things you told me that night at the party."

I swallow. I'd told him I liked him?

"And you told me you thought I wasn't serious about you, because I was about to go away, and because I'd recently come out of a two-year relationship, and because I'd never made a move"—*Fact,* I mentally tick the boxes off in my head—"and I told you why I hadn't."

I freeze. "And … why was that?" I chance a tentative glance at him, hopeful.

He shakes his head and gives a soft laugh. "It's … what matters is that we could make this thing work, Stacey. You just need to give it a chance."

He leans back against the bedhead with his hands behind his head, staring at the ceiling. I sigh and join him there. He thinks I'm embarrassed of him, when it couldn't be further from the truth. It's him who should be embarrassed of me.

What was …?

"Why is the bed moving?" I hiss at Michael. He's rocking back and forth with his legs, pushing against the headboard so the mattress moves back and forth ever so slightly.

"Ugh," he offers up what can only be described as the sort of grunt a cow might make while having sex. The mattress squeaks. He slams the palm of his hand against the headboard and looks at me, nodding, letting me know it's my turn.

I smile. "Harder!"

He gives me back a grin in return. A part of me melts. How can a guy have dimples that freaking sexy?

The bed squeaks as Michael rocks and hits the head of the bed, over and over.

"Try it," he whispers, jerking his head toward his hand. I scrunch up my nose.

I slap the headboard myself. That feels good. Really good.

"Do it again," he whispers. "Think about your family, being all crap and overachieving and stuff."

"Yes!" I scream.

Shae's moving out of home.

Slap.

It feels amazing.

"Now how 'bout how Dave is a dick for hurting your friend?" Michael grins.

"Yes!"

Slap.

"Yes!"

Life is unfair for making Kate so miserable.

Slap.

That stupid guy who put this baby inside me.

Slap.

Me.

Slap, slap, slap.

"Ugh!" Michael grunts again just as I give an almighty "yes" that I am sure will either have Kate putting on headphones or sending me a text telling me to can it.

There's something cathartic about slapping things. For the first time in one and a bit weeks, I feel a sense of peace wash over me.

I let out a contented sigh and lift the edge of the blankets, snuggling down underneath the quilt. Michael rests his head on the pillow, his body stretched next to mine. After a few moments, my breathing slows, returning to a normal rate. I turn to my side, facing away from Michael. He moves one tentative hand to rest on my waist.

I like the way it feels.

A lot.

"So that's what you sound like?" I look over my shoulder. One corner of his mouth rises in a smile.

"I sound better." I shuffle back so my body is pressed against his. He is warm.

Firm.

Nice.

"You know, you could always show me—"

"Hey! Don't ruin post-sex cuddles." I frown and wrap his arm around me tighter.

We lie there in silence for a few moments, me watching the bright lights still dancing around out the window, concentrating on his hot breath in my hair, behind my ear. He gives me goose bumps.

"You are the most confusing person I know," Michael whispers.

Ain't that the truth.

December 10

The warm sun beats down on my face. I open my eyes, fighting the stickiness that falling asleep while wearing mascara brings. I run my tongue along my teeth, the gross feeling of furry and—

Oh God.

Last night.

Michael.

I inch my leg behind me, hoping to feel his warmth. Maybe we can make this work, somehow. Michael seems to think we can.

One inch: warm bed sheets.

Two inches: the bed cools.

Three inches: nothing.

I flip over. His side of the bed is empty, the quilt pulled up, and the sheets tucked in, as if he had never even been there in the first place.

On his pillow lies a note, man-scrawl scratched across its surface in blue hotel-room pen.

I'll keep your secrets.
I just won't be one.

Ouch.

week five

December 17

NOTHING SAYS *I'm a glamorous eighteen-year-old who has just finished school* quite like lining up at the doctor's for the second time in a month. Because the pap smear wasn't enough. Ugh.

I take my phone from my handbag and click the screen on. Nope. Nothing. No new messages.

I don't know why I think there will be. I've been waiting for a text from Michael all week, but since I was the one who pushed him out the door, who made him think I was embarrassed of him? I guess it was really no wonder.

He's not good for me. I have bigger things to worry about.

Me: Why did the calf cross the road?

I hit send before I can stop myself. *What am I doing?* I've made it perfectly clear to Michael that I'm not interested, meaning I have him right where I want him.

So why am I sending him a text message?

Sometimes, you do something even when you know it's bad

for you. You break the rules; you indulge when it's forbidden. And as you do it you think, screw it, damn the man, I've got this—I *deserve* this. I get this one small thing as a reward for all my times of good and hard work. Then you remember you don't deserve shit. Because if you did, you wouldn't be paying for your rebellion right now.

At times like this, it's easy to become addicted to pain. Especially when it's self-inflicted.

I glance around at the six other people in the waiting room. There is an elderly couple; the woman clutches the man's arm as if she is afraid his skin will wrinkle up and drop to the floor. Well, more so than it has already.

Then there is a guy a little younger than me—sixteen, maybe?—and a woman who looks to be mid-thirties. This is a sexual health clinic, a free doctor service that deals with all things between the sheets—what problems do they have that call for a visit to the sexy doctors'?

I busy myself with imagining their problems while I wait my turn. Maybe mid-thirties lady is a porn star. And sixteen-year-old has a weird fetish for cotton wool, and wants to know if it is normal to wrap his penis—

My phone vibrates on my lap. I look down and smile. *Michael.*

Michael: To get to the udder side. You're gonna have to do better than that, Allison ...

I smirk. I guess that means he doesn't hate me, at least?

"Stacey Allison." A middle-aged man walks out into the waiting room from a poorly lit corridor behind him. At least it isn't the same guy who gave me the pap smear. *Must have rotating rosters.*

I stand up and sling my handbag over my arm, then follow the doctor down the hall into a small office. It is just like every other doctor's office I've ever been to: clean, full of medical equipment, the good ol' height-to-weight chart on the wall, and a model of a vagina. Well, okay, so maybe that wasn't in *every* doctor's office.

"Hi, I'm Dr Simpson." The doctor sits down in a chair next to his desk and gestures for me to take a seat on the one behind me. I oblige.

"I'm Stacey." I smile, then cringe. "Sorry, you already know that …"

Dr Simpson doesn't let my awkwardness fluster him. "So, what can I do for you today?" He smiles a thoroughly pleasant smile, the kind that makes me feel completely non-intimidated. *I hope cotton wool ball guy gets this doc, too.*

"Well, so …" I swallow. Oh yeah. This isn't a social call. "I think I'm pregnant. I mean, I am. Well, I did a test, and it said I was, so I kind of presume that it's most likely a foetus growing inside me."

The seconds tick on into what feels like hours as the doctor licks his lips, takes a deep breath—ew! He's a mouth breather—and then tilts his head to the side, studying me.

"And when was your last period?" He clasps his hands together over his crossed knee.

"It was …" I do the mental maths, and feel like that idiot girl in every pregnancy movie. You know the one. *Oh, how didn't I realise that my period is, like, ninety weeks late?*

"It should have started around seven weeks ago," I say. "So I'm kind of … three weeks late."

Damn idiot. I was an idiot.

"Right." The doctor pauses, scribbling some numbers on a chart. "Your periods are usually quite regular?"

"Yes."

"And when do you think you conceived?" He turns his head to look at me.

"About five weeks ago." I swallow.

"That would have put you at the peak ovulation period in your cycle." He nods, tapping his pen against his lip. "I'll get you to do a test, just to be sure, but yes, it certainly does sound like you are pregnant." The doctor jerks open a drawer and rifles through its contents until he finds a small plastic cup with a yellow lid.

"Here." He holds it out in my direction.

Oh God no. Please, no, don't make me—

"You'll need to urinate in this cup. Try and catch it mid-flow, not after the initial burst." He smiles and jiggles the cup a little, as if that will make it more appealing.

Again?

I take the cup and walk out of the room, my shoulders slumped, and head toward the toilet sign I'd seen down the hall. As I pass the reception area, I try to hide the plastic cup of shame in my pocket, but it's obvious what's happening. The elderly man gives me a knowing nod, and the middle-aged woman winks at me. You never just 'forget to go' before you see a doctor and have to break up your appointment to pee. This is a urine test, people.

I shut the door behind me, pull down my shorts, unscrew the lid on the cup and—

Nothing.

Waterfalls, rushing water, open taps …

Dry as a bloody desert.

I imagine the cup of coffee I'd sucked down this morning speeding through my throat, down into my stomach and my intestines or whatever the hell path liquid goes through, and filling up my bladder, all the way to the brim. I squeeze. I push.

Zero.

I wish I'd know there was going to be a pee test.

I stand up and waddle—well, my pants are around my knees—over to the sink where I wrench open the faucet and stick my head under the tap, drinking as much of the spewing water as I can. I gulp so much down I feel my stomach expanding, to the point where I could be sick.

Then, leaving the tap still running at full ball, I waddle my way back to the toilet, hover and try again.

After three minutes, I finally pee, and start the awkward *should I shove it under now/is this mid-stream enough* dance, followed quickly by the *where the hell is my pee and—crap it's on my hand* routine.

Altogether, the experience is rating very below par.

I finally wash my hands—four times—and head back to the doctor's office, pee cup firmly sealed. I cringe, trying to find a way to hold it so I can't feel how … *warm* the liquid is. *Shudder.*

"Here." I shove the cup of liquid onto the good doctor's desk and sit down, turning my head away. Something about seeing my pee makes me feel nauseous.

When I look back, I see Dr Simpson has opened the lid on my pee jar—ew!—and stuck a little thing in it. Looks like his pregnancy test is very similar to mine.

"May I ask, is this a planned pregnancy?" The doctor fishes around on his desk for a little mouse and right-clicks, bringing his computer to life.

"Not exactly, no." I shake my head. "Or at all, really."

He turns to me, and I swear, there is something like sympathy in his eyes. "Are you in a relationship with the father?"

"No." My voice is quieter this time.

"Do you know who the father is?"

"No," I squeak. My fingers fidget with each other on my knee.

Dr Simpson sighs, then leans over as if he is about to squeeze my hand, jerking his arm away at the last minute.

"Sorry, I—you remind me of my own daughter," he says. He turns back to his desk and grabs a blood pressure monitor. "I just need to take your blood pressure."

I thrust out my arm, and he wraps the Velcro material around it. "Just relax," he says, and I unclench my fist as he starts pumping that little balloon.

"So you're not sure who the father is. Could it be … one of multiple people?" Dr Simpson asks. My fingernails dive straight for my palms again. "Relax, please."

I want to say, *then stop asking me stressful questions!* Instead, I reply, "No. There's really only one."

"Well, that's a start. So you don't know who it is, but you know it's not say, one of five men." Dr Simpson nods, as if this is indeed a fact I am to be rewarded for. *Good work, Stacey.*

Only slutted yourself around to the one random guy. Nice to know.

"So, we'll need to get you checked for any diseases—"

"Done that." I nod, giving myself a mental high-five. "After it happened, I came in here and saw one of your other doctors, who gave me the tests. And I went to the pharmacist and got the morning-after pill. Which I, uh …" I fiddle with the hem of my shorts. "… kind of forgot to take."

"That'll do it," Dr Simpson says with a wink. I smirk. This guy is my kinda doctor.

"Doc, I've had four drinks since I would have fallen pregnant"—White lie. Technically, I had two beers the night before graduation, and four tequilas the week before. To help stave off the hangover—"and I was wondering, will this hurt …?"

"While we certainly do not recommend drinking while pregnant, and I'd encourage you to stop right away, this doesn't necessarily mean you'll have harmed the baby. Plenty of people don't realise they're pregnant and do things like that." Dr Simpson makes a few quick notes on his computer again, checks his little pee stick, then turns back to me. "It looks like you are indeed correct; you're with child."

The words hit me like a series of slaps to the face. Sure, I knew, but to have this guy with his clipboard and pen and a vial of my pee in a jar tell me? Now it's official.

I lean forward and rest my head in my hands. Why the hell has this happened to me?

"Well, that leaves us with one major question; have you thought about whether or not you will continue the pregnancy?" There's no judgment in Dr Simpson's eyes, only a kindly twinkle, which offers me a weird sense of comfort. Like maybe, no matter what I choose, it will be the right decision. The best decision.

"Listen, this is a huge choice for you. I don't know if you have certain religious preferences—"

"I don't."

"Well, regardless, termination is a very serious thing to

do. It's not what we call particularly traumatic surgery on the body—on the mind, though? Well, that can be a very different thing." He gives me a sad smile, and I press my lips together. I hadn't really thought about that.

"So it wouldn't … hurt too much?" I wince.

"No." Dr Simpson shakes his head kindly. "You would experience some discomfort, mind, and it's not what we'd call a pain-free experience by any means."

I nod.

"The other two major options we encourage people to consider at this point would be of course, having the baby and raising it, or having the baby and putting it up for adoption," he finishes.

"Adoption …" I trail off. Could I do that? Could I carry a living thing around, growing it in my stomach for nine whole months, get fat, give birth, potentially rip my vagina open, and then hand the kid over to someone else?

Could I kill it?

"I can't keep it. It's stupid to even …" I trail off, studying the pine-green carpet.

"Stacey," Dr Simpson leans closer, "it's a big decision. You don't need to make it today."

He shifts back in his seat and taps at his computer keyboard again, no doubt entering something like *Does not have a clue of plan.*

"I know you're uncertain of the child's paternity, but it's important you discuss this. We have a very good counsellor who works in the building; she'd be able to meet with you, if you'd like." He presses a final button on his keyboard and turns back to me. "And talk to your family about it. Discuss your options."

"That is not a good idea." I widen my eyes.

"Friends, then," he says. This time, I don't comment. How do I say that I really only have one super close female friend, and that she's going through a whole heap herself right now? And that the rest of the people I'd consider in my tight group are all guys, who I cannot, repeat, *cannot* tell I'm carrying some random dude's baby?

"Until you've decided whether you're going to have the baby or not, I'd recommend taking some folic acid supplements, just in case you do decide to continue with the pregnancy. I'd also recommend you adhere to the suggested dietary and nutrition guidelines—no alcohol, minimal caffeine, no soft cheeses, no raw fish, no—"

"Whoa, hold up, I need to write this down." I scrabble around in my handbag for a pen.

"It's fine, I have two websites to recommend for you that will detail all this, plus some brochures." Dr Simpson takes some pamphlets from a holder on the wall and places them in a brown paper bag for me. "I'll also get you to go in for a blood test, just to make sure you're all fit and healthy. How are you feeling?"

I swallow. *Blood test.* "Okay."

"No nausea or discomfort of any kind?"

"Not yet." My stomach rolls. *Well, not until you suggested it.*

"Just be aware that occasionally, morning sickness can start as early as five weeks, so you could very well be a candidate for that," he says. I do a mental cheer.

The printer whirrs into life and hums away, sucking the paper in and spitting it out. Dr Simpson gathers it, along with a few more brochures he selects from Perspex holders on the wall. Planned Pregnancy. Abortion & You. Adoption: The Greatest Gift. They're all there, right next to the ones on erectile dysfunction and sexual diseases.

I shudder. At least I'm not taking either of those home with me.

"Once you get the blood test, you can call in three days to get the results, but in the meantime, I'd be having a look through those brochures and thinking seriously about this. Talk to someone, Stacey."

Dr Simpson then proceeds to give me information on what to do if I keep the baby; things like my first ultrasound and tests at around twelve weeks, and birthing classes, although he assures me it's very early to worry about that.

When our time is up, I heave a sigh of resignation and push back in my chair then stand up, taking the little bag Dr Simpson hands me.

I shuffle out the door and hand over my Medicare card to the receptionist, surreptitiously glancing at the other patients still in the room.

"Benjamin Jones?" Dr Simpson asks. The sixteen-year-old guy gets to his feet.

I think I'd prefer the cotton wool problem.

Getting the needle hurts like getting a needle hurts, with an extra pinch of remorse and embarrassment thrown in. I drove to the next town to get it done, because the odds of me running into someone I knew in our local pathology centre were once again high, and I didn't know if there was some special doctor note that said *Look out, she's preggers* on my blood test form.

I'm driving home, ominous clouds lurking behind me as I speed down the motorway toward Lakes. I don't know why I'm driving fast. It's not like I have anything to rush home for, anything to rush home to. All I can think about is this baby. And what the hell I'm going to do about it.

Who the hell I can talk to?

I swallow. There's one other person out there who probably doesn't want to hear from me right now, but I think they should. After all, I need to talk this through. And I don't want to do it alone.

I take the exit for Lakes, the series of suburbs where I live. Now, the rain is pouring down, one of those gross tropical summer storms where it drenches your socks off and then heats up, leaving you feeling as if you're an extra cast member on *Lost* or something.

After another twenty minutes, I get to the point where

I remember Michael picking me up. The rain has stopped, thank God.

Before I exit the car, I check my phone. One new message.

Michael: Why did the man put condoms on his ears during sex?

I shake my head. Like I have a freaking clue. Grabbing my skateboard from the backseat, I open my door and step out into the chaos after quickly typing out, *I don't know.*

I put my board down and start rolling. I'll be able to cover more ground on wheels, but I don't want to search in my car, in case someone tries to run me down for driving at the speed of an old lady. My eyes are wide open for anything that looks familiar. I still can't believe my luck. How is it that the one time I am too drunk to remember to be careful, I get pregnant?

Okay, so it's not exactly immaculate conception, but seriously. My brother Sean and his wife had been trying for a kid for three years. They'd done IVF, crazed diet fads ... the works, and it was only a few months ago now that they finally managed to conceive. And here I am, a dumb kid who got too drunk to remember having sex, let alone using protection, and officially pregnant. The guy must have been some kind of a super sperm machine.

I put one foot down and push myself along, the hum of the wheels on the pavement a soundtrack to my search. My head flicks from right to left as I observe all the houses I pass. They all look perfectly presentable—modern homes, with well-manicured lawns, and warm yellow light reflected against their windows.

None of them look like the den of a sperm machine. No particularly masculine scents waft from any of the windows.

I roll and I roll, and after a while they all look familiar; they all look like I could have been in them before, and I just as easily could have not.

After an hour of street searching, I turn around and trudge back to my car. I throw my skateboard on the front seat, watching it crush the paper bag of brochures Dr Simpson gave me.

My phone buzzes.

Michael: He didn't want to get hearing aids.

Oh.

week six

December 19

WHEN I was a kid, I always used to dream about being older.
I'd follow Sean around, begging him to let me ride my bicycle with him and his mates down the bush track to the creek.

I'd sneak into Shae's room while she was on the phone then quickly bolt back out again when she threw her pillow at me. I'd even try look under the door when I knew she had a boy in there.

I wanted to shave my legs at aged ten, but Mum wouldn't let me. I did it anyway.

I had my first alcoholic drink at age thirteen. It was a sip of Sean's beer. I hated it, but drank it regardless.

I've always wanted to grow up a whole heap faster than was really possible. I always pretended to be older than I was.

Now I wish I'd slowed it down.

Now, I'm pregnant and sitting on the couch in the most unladylike fashion imaginable, legs spread out, hand behind my head. A giant bowl full of popcorn sits on my stomach.

Sat.

Now it's more like three kernels of popcorn.

Comfort eating does wonders for the soul.

"Could you close your legs?" Shae asks as she gracefully glides into the room. I'm not even sure her feet touch the ground.

I snap my knees together, pulling my feet in front of me. "It's not like I'm wearing a skirt," I mutter, even though I know she's right. I'm not a little kid anymore, no matter how much I'm trying to act like one.

Shae walks over to my side and places herself on the edge of the couch, as far away as she can get from me without actually sitting somewhere else. And, since the curtains Mum is hemming are on the other two lounges in the room, Shae really doesn't have a whole heap of choice.

"What are you watching?" She gives me a pointed look. One that says *Please say something else.*

I throw her the remote in reply. I can't focus anyway.

She flicks through the stations and settles on a news channel; not the commercial kind, mind you, but the government broadcast ones. You know, extra dry, where the weather comes to you from a politician's house instead of the zoo.

I turn to study my sister. Her hair is falling perfectly around her face, the right amount of wave for a casual Monday-night dinner, which she is, of course, ready an hour early for. She has on a tiny amount of makeup, and even though her clothes look casual, I know for a fact they're designer.

She's so put together; so perfect. She *looks* like a grown-up.

I think back to the times when she'd talk on her phone in her bedroom, when I'd spy on her having boys over.

Even as a teenager, she'd been on top of things.

"Hmph," Shae sighs.

"What's up?" I grab a pillow and hug it to my stomach.

"Just this crisis in Syria ..." She shakes her head, as if the weight of the world is upon her. "So tragic."

I start to compose a list in my head.

Things That Are Worse Than Being Pregnant.

Being involved in a war crisis in Syria.

"Mmm." I nod.

"Do you know how many people have died because of this?" She turns and focuses those crystal-blue eyes on me, and I swear they can see into my soul. "How many children?"

Children, children, children …

Okay, so the word might not really have echoed in my head, but it sure as hell felt like it did. Was I going to murder a child, too? Would that put me on Syria level in my sister's eyes?

"Are there many … kids … in Syria?" I ask, trying to search for a clue as to how she'd react to my news.

"Stacey." Shae rolls her eyes. "Of course there are. Have you ever watched the news?"

I shrug and pick at the corner of the cream-coloured pillow. It's starting to thread at the seam.

"Course," I mutter, focused on my task at hand.

"Sometimes I wonder …" She turns her attention back to the television just as an ad break comes on. "So have you thought any more about what you're going to do next year?"

I bust out that list in my mind again.

2. Having to discuss future career plans with my sister.

I lift my gaze and study Shae once more. She's turned her face to me, so I can see the pointed look she's throwing me, and it takes everything inside me not to open up the cushion I'm holding and try and hide inside it with the stuffing. Why is she on the attack tonight?

"Not really." *Just get a job at the supermarket, or maybe as a cleaner. Oh, or have a baby. You know, nothing special.*

"Is it hard?" Her brow creases, and for a second I think she's being sympathetic to my cause. Because yes; sometimes, being the only dumb-arse with four high-achieving siblings *is* hard. Because not being dux of the school, or being president of anything bar the social committee isn't considered that worthwhile in my family.

"Honestly … I'm kind of freaked out." I bite my lip. "What am I going to do?"

"You can go to TAFE." Shae smiles, and gives me a light punch on the shoulder. "Or if that's too hard, you could work a checkout. And, hey! You could be a hairdresser. No one trims my fringe like you do."

The words warm my heart. I have zero interest in being a hairdresser—people's scalps gross me out—but it's nice to hear my sister tell me she thinks I can do something.

"Speaking of, would you mind giving me a trim after dinner? I have my one-year work anniversary dinner tomorrow!" Shae all but squeals, and of course I smile and nod. Her motivation is exposed, but what else can I do?

"Girls, will you help me with a few things in the kitchen?" Mum calls from the next room.

"Stace can do it. I've got a big week coming up with work," Shae yells back. I raise my eyebrows at her.

"I'll pay you for the trim." She widens her eyes, like I'm being a baby.

Maybe I am.

Maybe it's just 'cause I have one growing inside me.

I stir the vegetables around my plate, making little shapes, little faces of peas and carrots and potato. I don't hear a word my family says. I see their mouths opening, take note of the smiles, the laughter, the puffed-up chests and the fork-to-mouth action.

But all I hear are two things.

My sister's confidence in my checkout chick career.

And the voice inside of me asking what the hell I'm doing with this baby.

"Can I please be excused?"

I don't wait for an answer, just push my chair back and walk calmly to the stairs. My stomach is churning, as if a bowling ball is rocking around on a bed of liquid in there.

What the hell am I going to do? The sad thing is—the thing I *hate* to admit—even if I get an abortion, my life is screwed. I'm not going to get into uni, and even if I do, can I really break the mould? Can I be anything *but* Stacey the checkout chick, Stacey the socialite, *Stacey the only disappointment in the Allison household*?

I throw myself down on my bed, staring at my white ceiling, the posters on my walls of all the movie stars I liked when I was thirteen. When I was still a kid.

At least then I didn't feel so alone. Sure, I was always rushing to grow up, but people still ... well, they didn't treat me like I was on this predestined path to Dumb-ArseVille.

I squeeze my eyes shut, trying to ignore the heat building underneath my lids. *Eff off, tears. Go away.*

What if this baby is the one thing I could do right? The one thing I could own, that would love me unconditionally?

I shake my head. I'm being an idiot.

If only there was someone I could talk to about all of this ...

I've always been popular. I've never had any shortage of people willing to share in my deepest, darkest secrets.

Now, I feel desperately alone.

Some secrets you just can't share.

Me: I'm sorry.

I hit send and wait for the reply. Of course, it doesn't come straight away, and I chide myself for checking that my phone isn't on silent. Three times.

I've almost drifted off to sleep when the phone dings right next to my ear, sending me flying upright.

Michael: What for?

I sigh. What does he mean what for? He's the one who left *me* the note.

But maybe this is a good thing. Maybe he's ready to forgive, to forget. I smile as I type out my response.

> **Me: For being a bitch to you in Surfer's. And for eating the last chocolate.**
>
> **Michael: ??**
>
> **Me: Next time we hang out, you'll see.**

This time, the wait is longer. I lick my lips, my eyes glued to the screen.

> **Michael: Next time, hey? Well, I can be cool with that. So tell me, how's tricks back in Lakes?**
>
> **Me: No doubt not as exciting as they are on tour with Coal! Any girls throw their underwear at you yet?**
>
> **Michael: No more than usual. And when they do, they're usually aiming for Dave.**

I grin as I relax back into my pillows again, enjoying having this ridiculously normal and kind of boring conversation. He's someone I can talk to. He's someone who doesn't think I'm just some slutty bimbo.

He's someone who is touring the country with the world's hottest rock band, and couldn't be there for his pregnant girlfriend. Especially since the kid isn't even his.

> **Me: Hey Michael?**
>
> **Michael: Yeah?**
>
> **Me: Can I ask you something random?**
>
> **Michael: Is it if I think you're cute? Coz …**

I open and close the message icon on my phone at least fifty times in the space of a minute.

> **Michael: You know you're the cutest thing I've ever seen.**

Heat rushes to my cheeks and I smile. What the hell is wrong with me? Guys have told me they think I'm sexy. I've had roses delivered to my damn class for Valentine's Day three years running and this—one message from a guy, saying I'm cute, something you'd call a teddy bear—has me blushing?

I shake my head. I need to snap out of it.

> **Me: So ... you know how I don't know what I'm going to do next year?**

> **Michael: Are you going to be an actor, Miss Number One?**

I pause. Honestly, I hate the idea. Drama sounds so intense, too much pressure on your career to get the part, to make it big. If only I could practice drama and acting every day, without actually having to go through the rehearsals stage ...

> **Stacey: I think it's too much pressure.**

> **Michael: What about teaching it?**

The message comes through so quick that my shoulders jerk in surprise. He had an answer already?

He's thought about me. About my future.

I blink. Teaching is something I've honestly never thought of before. I try the word on for size in my brain. *Teaching.* I could do that. I mean, I'd have to do a bridging course, and study like a mo-fo to get the grades, but I could. I could so totally do that.

All of a sudden, my line of questioning changes.

> **Me: I actually like that idea. A lot.**

> **Michael: Great! Whatcha gonna do next year problem = solved.**

> **Me: Yeah, well I'll have to do a bridging course, and apply for a midyear intake. If I even get in.**

Suddenly, I'm filled with excitement for this idea. I'd love to teach drama, even if it only seems like a pipe dream at this point.

A pipe dream I may never achieve, thanks to …

> **Me: Anyway … so, there's a puppy. And it doesn't have anyone else to care for it, and while I can choose if I look after it or not, I know taking care of this thing will really impact my career and studies.**

But I probably wont get in to a course anyway …

And it would be kinda nice to have something that depended on me, that I could look after … you know? So I should probably choose the puppy, right?

I hold my breath, count to twenty, and when Michael hasn't replied I throw the phone down on the bed. I can't believe I'm asking him this, but it's the closest I can come without—well, without seeing the sad look in his eyes I know would be there if he found out.

> **Michael: What, is it at a shelter or something?**

I groan, and thump my head against the pillow.

> **Me: Yep. But I'm the only one who can take it.**

I pause for a moment.

Me: Or they'll kill it.

As soon as I type the words, a wave of guilt floods over me. Now I have to add hypothetical puppy murderer to my list of sins.

How will killing a baby feel?

Michael: I think you could do uni and a puppy. I really don't think you need to choose.

I press my lips together and turn away from the phone. So maybe my hypothetical situation wasn't so great after all. If I want to talk to someone about this, I'll really have to talk to someone about this. Baby and all.

I roll over onto my side, my stomach still feeling like jelly is rolling around in it.

Michael: I guess what you need to ask yourself is, how much do you love this puppy? And what can it give you?

Can you live with yourself if it dies and you know you could have saved it?

His words sink in, and I don't. I don't know if I can live with that. Not when there are people I know and love who have had to try for a baby and who had difficulty conceiving, like my brother and his wife. Not when I've always tried so hard to look after other living creatures, and sought out the grown-up lifestyle so vividly. Not when it would mean I'd be a murderer, someone who killed this small person inside of me.

I reread Michael's text, my eyes focusing on the second last line, this time.

Not when it could give me love. It could depend on me.

God, sometimes I just want someone to depend on me.

Someone to know that I love them and for that to be enough.

I roll over onto my back and stare at the ceiling, my phone on the pillow beside me. I wish there was someone I could talk to about this, but I can't burden Kate, and the idea of talking to my family …

I could talk to the counsellor, the one the doctor suggested. But how the hell could I afford to pay for that? Air puffs out from between my lips and I shake my head. Yep, that's me. The girl who is considering paying someone to be her friend.

"Stace, five minutes till trim time!" Shae calls through the door. I sit up, and hug my knees to my chest. Just no. I can't tell them yet, anyway.

If I could write a letter to myself in six years from now, what would I write? What would I want to hear?

But it's not about me.

It's about the baby.

I reach over and slide the pen and notepad from my desk, opening the book up to a fresh page. I purse my lips together for a few moments before I begin.

> Dear Baby
>
> So, I'm your mum. You probably already know this, because if you can read, then you are alive and at least older than … say …

I pause, and quickly Google average reading ages on my phone.

> … five-ish But apparently if you're only able to read this when you're eight, that's okay too, because everyone is different.

I bite my lip. What if my child is slow? And people tease

her? Or worse—what if people like her? And by people, I of course mean boys.

I take a deep breath and nod. She's not even born yet. And she might be a he.

I'm going to be the best mum you could have I promise to look after you, and love you, and I'll never forget your birthday. Ever.
I know it's a while in the future now, but when it comes time for you to leave school, I'm going to be there for you, too, helping you make the right choices Because you know what? It's fu freaking scary out there No one tells you what the right answers are for your life, you know?
Take you, for example I can't talk to anyone about you, but I think—I know the right thing to do is to give you a chance

I shake my head, thinking of Shae's dismissal of me earlier in the day.

Everyone deserves a chance.
And I have a secret. I already know you're going to save me You're going to be the one thing I'm good at.
I can't wait to give you the world, baby

Love,

Sta
MUM

The jelly that was loitering in my stomach before flips over and becomes scrambled jelly eggs, only this time they're clawing their way up my throat, desperate to get out.

Excess saliva fills my mouth, followed by the sting of acid, that vile, lemon-gone-wrong taste that you know means one thing, and one thing only.

"Stace! Are you ready to do my hair?" Shae yells outside my door, but I have no time.

She flings the bedroom door open as I bolt for my en-suite bathroom.

"Hey!" she yells.

By that stage, I'm already heaving my guts up, all over the toilet seat.

I scrunch my mental list up into a little ball and accept facts.

Pregnancy sucks.

December 20

Michael: Are you at home right now?

I look down at my baggy yoga pants and tank top. Well yes, I'm at home right now. In fact, I'm almost embarrassed at how at home I am. Because I am …

Knitting.

Yes, I know.

Knitting.

It's something I never thought I'd do, but since the morning sickness started and this whole "You're seriously about to have a baby" thing kicked in, I've wanted to try doing something … well, maternal-ish. And knitting was the easiest option, since I could hardly try and barrel my mother out of the kitchen.

So far, I've managed to knit three inches of one scarf. And ruined four balls of wool.

But who's counting? What matters is that by the time I have this child, he'll have handmade winter clothes for days.

Whoa. By the time …? When did that happen?

I look back at my phone, and my hand is hovering over the *send* button on the *No* text I've tapped out, when there's a knock on my bedroom door.

"Stacey?" Mum asks. I shove my knitting underneath my hot pink comforter, cringing once more at how embarrassing it is to have a princess bedroom as an eighteen-year-old.

"Yes?"

"You have a guest at the door," she replies. I furrow my brows in confusion. I stand up, just as Mum swings my bedroom door open. "He says to bring a pair of flip flops."

What?

And that's how I end up in a car again with Michael, yet another bad idea in my recent spate of them.

"And you won't tell me where we're going?" I tilt my head.

"Nope." He shakes his, his eyes firmly fixed on the road in front of him.

"But obviously it's out of Lakes …" I trail off as we enter the motorway leading from our hometown to Sydney.

"Yep." Michael nods as he overtakes a semitrailer and the vintage car kicks up a gear, hitting the speed limit with a slight cough and splutter.

We drive in silence for a while. I watch the cars flash past my window, and Michael is no doubt concentrating on keeping the shuddering engine inside the bonnet.

"Aren't you supposed to be on tour?" I ask for the third time since he came to my door. Dave & The Glories tour with Coal was a two-month stint. They were in Australia until the start of January, and Michael should have been on the road with them.

"Stacey, Stacey, Stacey," Michael shakes his head. "It's a Tuesday. No one in rock 'n' roll works on a Tuesday."

"Did a show get cancelled?"

"Yeah, a show got cancelled. Dave's having some drama with the lead singer of Coal. Hit on his girlfriend, or something." He shifts uncomfortably in his seat.

My blood boils as I think about that idiot. Of course he's gone after some other guy's girl. Of course …

But wait. If they were supposed to play a gig, doesn't that mean—

"Doesn't that mean you were interstate this morning, flew back, and will have to travel somewhere tomorrow?" I furrow my brow.

Silence.

"Well … yes, I guess you could look at it like that." Michael slowly nods. "But also my mum was missing me, and I had some … stuff I had to do back here, so …"

I smile. I want to fight it, but the damn sucker of a grin works its way up my face and over my cheeks. "And so if you have all this stuff on, why are you visiting me?"

Michael sucks in a breath. His eyes narrow, and he presses his lips together.

Then he puts his hand on my knee.

And even though this is a guy who I know I can't have because I have a baby, and he's in a band, and I don't even know if he's really that into me …

I like it. It sends tingles up through my core and I really, *really* like it.

Silence washes over us for the rest of the hour-long car trip. But his hand stays on my knee. And my heart stays in my throat.

Finally, we park on the street in the inner city, near Surry Hills, I think. Michael gets out of the car and runs around to my side where he wrenches the door open before I can get to it.

"Thanks." I smile. It makes the lack of his heat on my knee a little more bearable.

He puts his hand on the small of my back and guides me down the road. We walk on the bitumen pavement past high-rise brick office buildings, past modern cafes with herb gardens out the front and past tiny parks with men sleeping— their bellies exposed by their flannelette shirts and cardboard signs by their sides requesting money.

Sydney. It's high, and it's low.

We reach an old church. Its steeples spike high into the cloudy late-afternoon sky overhead, and its mass stretches out to a quadrangle beside the main cathedral. Michael steps forward and unlatches the iron gate, opening it up.

"After you." He sweeps his hand forward.

Of course, this is when my stupid Christian guilt decides to kick in. I freeze on the spot. My mum raised all of us kids as Catholics, even though we haven't worshipped in a long while. Now here I am, on the steps of a church, and I'm unwed and pregnant to a guy I don't know.

At least I'm keeping the baby.

This time, the voice doesn't surprise me. I just smile. It's what I'm doing. I'm keeping. I made it, and I'll keep it safe.

I inch a step forward. Lightning doesn't strike me down, so I take another. So far, so good.

"So, you're taking me to church?" I ask. Vines creep up the walls of the building, reaching for the sun like the loyal to the lord.

"Not exactly." Michael laughs, a deep rumbling sound that gives me the same feeling between my legs that him putting his hand on my knee did. Why is it that now that I know I can't have him, I want him even more? Or is this just crazy pregnancy hormones?

He leads me farther forward, then swings to the right of the main church building. We enter the quadrangle through a vine-covered archway, and then he turns to the right, leading us toward a room at the far right of the area with a typed sign out front:

The Actor's Handbook

I know the name. It's one of the city's top three drama schools. Our high school tutor told us about this place, speaking of its expensive but worthwhile classes and the prestige of being accepted there into a full-time course.

"What the hell …?" I say the words as I think them. What is he playing at, taking me here?

"So … I know you said you were kind of interested in teaching acting, right?" Michael turns to me, a hopeful grin on his face. Something inside of me churns. He spent money on enrolling us into a class at this place?

"Yes …" I swallow. "One day, in the future, maybe …" *Maybe after I've had this child and gotten some sort of degree, if I am even eligible …*

"Well … we're doing an acting class this evening. Surprise."

My stomach rolls over and I instinctively clutch at it. *Not now, random five o-clock sickness.*

"Michael, I'm not really prepared …"

He looks me up and down. "You look pretty prepared to me."

For the third time today, I curse myself for answering the door in sweat pants. What the hell was I thinking?

"I can't …" I shake my head again. I have no words. No words except *no*. "I'll pay you back for your deposit, or whatever this costs. I just, I can't." I cringe, thinking of the money going out the window. Money I will need.

"Look, Stacey, this is how it is." Michael squares his shoulders to mine. "You go in, you do the class. I've already paid. We're attending students." He sucks in a deep breath. It makes me look at his lips. *His lips …* "You leave. We go grab a bite and go home. Three, four hours of your life, including travel time, max."

I lick my lips. How can I tell him that I can't possibly, I'm not brave enough, I couldn't try to show myself to these people who pretend for real?

Michael places his hands on my shoulders.

"Yes."

I have no hesitation.

We walk into the room, and my first thought is, *we are the youngest ones here.* Everyone else looks to be in his or her late twenties to early thirties. They are talking with each other while stretching—one girl is even wearing a leotard.

"Are you sure this is—"

"It's a thing." Michael takes my handbag from my shoulder and puts it down underneath an unoccupied bench space behind us. I sit on the seat, twisting my fingers in knots around each other. The nerves are eating me up.

"Hi." A man in black sweat pants that could be cousins with my own comes bouncing up to us. "You must be Michael and Stacey." His gaze flicks to the clipboard in his hand, then back up at us.

"Hey." Michael thrusts out a hand for him to shake, but the guy laces his fingers between Michael's, then pulls Michael's knuckles up to his mouth for a delicate kiss.

Michael's cheeks turn tomato red, and he takes his hand back super slowly—too slowly. So slow that I think our teacher might have ideas, even though I have no doubt Michael was only delaying his hand retraction so as not to seem rude.

"I'm Stacey." I thrust my hand under our tutor's nose, and he gives it a limp pump before turning his attention back to Michael.

"I'm Amon. We start in two minutes. I just need you to sign this waiver"—He flicks over a page on the clipboard and shoves it under our noses. I shoot a nervous glance at Michael, but he signs our lives away. Who knew acting was a high-risk activity?—"and then when you've completed any stretching you want to do, I encourage you to join us in the centre of the room." Amon offers up a sweeping bow and departs, frolicking off to a crowd of other people who no doubt come here every week.

"This is what you're doing to get me pumped about my future?" I scrunch my nose up.

"This is what you *are* doing, because you're excited about your future." Michael taps my nose, pushing the crinkles away and I laugh. It's one of the first genuine things I've done for a while.

"Okay people …" Amon claps his hands and the other eight people in the room amble toward him. "Welcome to Tuesday's class, improv. Now today we have two new people in the room, Michael"—I swear he bats his eyelashes—"and Stacey. Michael, Stacey, want to tell us why you're here?"

I swallow. Who knew acting classes would be so much like AA?

"I'm here because Stacey—her" —Michael jerks a thumb my way—"is going to be a great actor or acting teacher one day. And I want to support her."

The nine people in the room burst into applause. One guy on Michael's right even claps him on the back. It's clearly the right answer.

"And you, Stacey? You're an actress-to-be?" Amon asks.

Heat flushes to my cheeks, straight from my belly, covering my neck. Nine sets of eyes turn to study me. I take a step back, flinching under their gaze. There is something so very different about doing well in school to doing well in life.

"I like acting …" I nod. Oh God, kill me. Please? "And so I came." I offer up a smile. I feel *I was forced to come* probably wont sit well amongst the acting elite.

Apparently, I needn't have worried. My answer didn't sit well regardless. One girl standing opposite me offers up a few tentative golf claps until she realises no one else is playing. Then she stops.

"Okay, welcome. So we're going to start off with some exercises designed to get in touch with your spiritual side. I want everyone to sit cross-legged in a circle." Amon instructs, and one by one, everyone plops to the floor in a circle around him. It's all very Zen, very yoga.

"Should we hold hands?" I ask Michael quietly, and giggle.

"I was getting to that," Amon hisses. Apparently I wasn't quiet enough. "Hold hands with the people on either side of you, and concentrate on your energy. Force out the good through one hand, and feel the positive energy being pumped through you with the other; then take the bad through your feet. Our energy is circling amongst us. Picture yourself as a slate being cleaned, a needle injecting the negative from your life. An empty blackboard ..."

"Do you think they give this talk before you get a colonoscopy?" Michael whispers.

I can't help it. I choke on my laughter.

"Is something funny, Miss Allison?" Amon glares at me. I bite my lip. Of course he knows my last name and is using it to correct me. How *teacher* of him.

"Uh-uh." I shake my head. Nothing at all.

"Hmm." He shoots one last *look* at me before blinking, and his eyes are the perfect picture of Zen once more. "Okay, so now we're going to work on focusing in on our inner light. For it's only once we look deep insides ourselves ..."

Amon drones on and on, and I drop hands with Michael and Sweaty Palms on the other side of me. Michael leans closer, so close I can feel the heat from his body hovering over my arm. "You're ... having fun?"

It's all I can do not to snort again. But he did pay, and I don't want to be rude, so I look up at him and nod. "Mmmmm."

"Now, I want you to all stand and sing the note deep inside of you, the note that is your very soul," Amon says, and he staggers to his feet, as if he's possessed by the spirit of religious clichés. "Reach out to your heart note and sing it; sing it for me."

We all stand, and then one by one, people are drop to their knees, humming weird, unharmonious notes that jar against my mind. My stomach lurches, and I clasp it, urging it to chill the hell out.

Michael gives me a look, and I shrug. "Your idea," I whisper.

He rolls his eyes and dramatically falls to his knees, clutching his heart as if he has just been shot. I snort.

Amon's eyes flash open. "Miss Allison?"

"Yes. Sorry." I drop down to my knees and place my forefinger and thumb in an om-like position.

"Are you searching for your inner tune?" Amon prompts. *I'm searching for my inner desire not to barf on your floor?*

Silence engulfs the room for several moments. The inner-voice love has stopped. I think I broke the melody.

"Okay, everybody up." I push up to my feet. I know the small human inside me weighs less than ... I search around the room ... a piece of chalk, but seriously, it feels like standing with her in me takes extra effort.

Her?

"All right class, Stacey, here, has trouble with trust. We're going to play the leaning game. Gather in a circle," Amon says, and students gather in a group that I am the centre of. Interesting.

"Turn around," Amon says, and I face away from him. Seconds later, a thick piece of material is lowered over my eyes, pressing tight and knotted behind my head.

"You are blindfolded," Amon says. *No shit, Sherlock.* "Now, you will lean back, and let the group take your weight. Trust us; fall as far as you can. We will catch you, no matter what. We are *here*."

I smile, but it's all lip, no eyes. What does he mean *trust them?*

"Just lean back, Stacey," Amon repeats.

I focus my weight on the balls of my feet and start to tilt my body backward. Surely Michael would catch me, right? I mean, even if the rest of these people won't—

Why is no one catching me?

My heart leaps to my throat and I stick a foot out behind me, steadying myself and standing upright. I wrench the blindfold off and spin to face the group, my heart pounding erratically.

I can see the disappointment in Amon's eyes. "Stacey, Stacey." He sighs. "Let's try again."

I press my eyes shut even tighter and cover them once more, trying to relax my lips, which are unnaturally tight, all of a sudden. I can do this. I can.

I lean my weight backward again, my fingernails digging trenches into my palms. I get to the point where my natural balance is lost and I'm falling. I'm falling. Holy shit, I'm gonna hit the floor.

I'm going to hurt my baby.

I strike out with my foot once again, and this time it's not just Amon who sighs. I'm no doubt about to win the Favourite Class Member award.

"Come on, Stacey." Amon's hands plonk down on my shoulders. He smells like garlic and incense. My stomach lurches, and even though I don't want to be sick in public, being sick on Amon doesn't sound horrid. I take very tiny breaths in. "You can do this. We will not let you fall. An essential part of acting is learning to trust your fellow troupe."

He removes his hands and his feet pad back to their original position. "One more time. You got this, Stacey."

I suck in a deep breath, letting the air fill through my nostrils, down my throat, inflating my lungs. They wouldn't let me fall. There would be all sorts of legal ramifications … although we did sign a waiver upon entry …

I lean back for the third time. I go past my normal centre of gravity where I feel comfortable, and I'm falling, I'm falling, oh my God, I have to save the—

Hands support my weight. Some are on my shoulders, some are my arms, my waist. One is uncomfortably close to my boobs, but I'm prepared to look past that. I'm safe.

I stand up, shrugging the hands away, and wrap my arms protectively around my stomach. My heart is rocketing against my chest and my breath is coming short and sharp. Do I have a problem with trust? *Is that what I was drinking … to run away from?*

With one arm still wrapped around me, I wrench the blindfold from my eyes. I spin around. Everyone is smiling, a few people even offering up cheers at my success. Only, I don't feel successful. I feel like the worst mother in the world.

What if I'd fallen and somehow injured the baby?

"See? Wasn't so hard, was it?" Amon takes the blindfold from my trembling hand. "Stacey?" He studies my face, pressing his thin lips together. "We're going to take a twenty-minute break, everyone." He claps his hands. "I'll see you back here at half past five."

Michael's hand is on my shoulder, squeezing. "Stace … you all right?"

"Fine." I face him, trying my hardest to make my face light. Gosh, why am I freaking out about this? It was just a stupid game.

"Let's go sit outside." With his hand on the small of my back again, he leads me into the courtyard and we sit on a stone bench hidden in an alcove right near the entrance. Cars zoom past, beeping their horns, and somewhere in the distance a child sings, some nursery rhyme that does little to lift my spirits.

"You wanna talk about it?" He puts his hand on my leg.

His hand, his hand is warm, and it sends those tingles through my body again. I'm so lost and confused, and when he leans closer, his lips close to mine, his eyes flaming with lust, I give in.

Gently, his soft, full lips press against my own. He smells of cologne and *man*, and I can't help but offer a subtle groan as he parts his mouth and delicately runs his tongue over my bottom lip. Sparks shoot through me, and I wrap my arms around his neck, reveling in the feel of his firm body pressed against my soft one.

Our lips come together hungrily, full of desire. He pulls me closer, one hand on the back of my head, fisting my hair as his tongue seeks entry into my mouth. This is no slow, romantic dance; it's passion, and need and desire all at once. It's everything I need, though I know I shouldn't have it. It makes me feel whole.

Lips still furiously locked, I slide a leg over his body and shift my weight, straddling him. I run my hands over his shoulders, feeling his broad muscles underneath his shirt, the way they tense against my touch.

He moves his hand from my waist higher to cup my breast. In my thin sweater, my nipple responds to his touch instantly, stiffening as he fuels my desire. He is so hard that I can feel it through my sweats. I rock against him, lost in the moment, lost in this.

I've wanted this for so long.

"Stacey," he breathes, pulling back. I ignore his warning and learn forward, pressing my lips against his, but this time when I try to slide my tongue in his mouth, his lips are firm. I try again, but they're unyielding. Nothing.

"Stace." His hands move to my hips and he pushes me back. I bite my lip. "Stace, do you remember what I told you that time? At the party?"

I gaze up at the white fluffy clouds scudding through the sky above us. Why does it all come down to that stupid party?

"No." I shake my head.

He breathes and licks his lips. "Well … I'm a virgin."

I blink. He's a virgin? What does that have to do with anything? And what his ex—"But what about Hannah?"

"Hannah … God, this sounds so lame. I didn't want to have sex with Hannah."

What? He didn't sleep with *Hannah?* I think of the short, blonde dancer who even I knew was supposed to be good for her, erm, flexibility in bed. Her pick-up line was 'I can do the splits.' If they didn't have sex, it had to be Michael's choice. "But …" I furrow my brow. "Why?"

"Because I wanted my first time to be with someone who mattered, Stace. Someone I really liked."

I nod. So I'm pregnant, and he's a virgin. Fabulous.

"That's why I didn't try anything those last few months at school. Because I knew you were not … you know … and I didn't think you'd be interested. Plus, I did kind of tell you how gorgeous I thought you were, *all the time*—"

"But you never made a move!" I pull back.

"You never made one, Stace. Look at you." He presses his body back farther against the seat and I shuffle my way to his side. I miss the feeling of him beneath me already. "You're like this freaking babe, who is popular, and funny, and smart—"

"Hah!"

"You are, Stacey. And I'm just this idiot guy in a band who hasn't even been laid." He clasps his hands together and leans forward, studying the cracked pavement in front of us. "You never took a chance on us."

I look at him. I study his dark hair, the lean muscles lining his shoulders, and I know. He is a truly decent guy, who is embarking upon a life filled with truly decent things.

I know that this can be the last time we hang out.

"Look, Michael. Today has been fun" —*and your kisses were amazing*—"but you can't keep coming back to see me anymore. You're in a band"—*and have zillions of hot, non-pregnant girls on tour*—"and I can't imagine getting back here is cheap. We should just head home"—*actually, also because I'm hungry, and that means I might spew again*—"and then we should just, cool it, yeah? You and I ... we're never going to work."

Because I'm pregnant. You have always been better than me.

And you're never going to be a part of my world.

The car ride home is one silent hour of torture. All I have to do is look at Michael's face to see the pain in his eyes; it's etched for the world to see. It stings knowing I'm the one who put that hurt there, and that it's mirrored in my heart, too.

Just pretend, Stacey.

Just pretend.

Dear Small Human,

You'll be proud to know I'm going to

cut my sister's hair, and I'm doing it for you.

During the past few weeks, I've been thinking a lot about our life together. Where we're gonna live. How we're gonna get by.

I know I'll have to tell Mum and Dad—your grandma and grandpa—soon, and I guess we'll live here for the first year or so, till we can find a place of our own. In the meantime, I'll try and find a job, raise some money—and cut my sister's hair.

I have to.

You're counting on me.

And God, am I counting on you. Right now, I'm alone. I am so alone that it scares me sometimes, and I just don't see a way out.

You're going to change all that.

You'll love me ... won't you?

Mum xx

December 25

"Merry Christmas!" Mum raps her knuckles on the door to my room and I squint my eyes open.

"Merry Christmas," I mutter. The ceiling above me is white,

littered with all those glow-in-the-dark stickers that little kids love. It's a mixture of My Little Pony and the universe; before me, Shae had this room. It's not hard to guess which of those stickers belonged to her.

I throw back my ridiculously childish quilt and swing my legs out of bed, whooshing out a deep breath of air as I do. I swallow down my saliva, hoping that today will be a break from the vomit. Thank God I have my own bathroom. Otherwise, I can't imagine how I'd hide the morning sickness from my over-the-top family.

Before I get up, I reach under my pillow, assessing the packet of Cheese & Onion chips there and the grated cheese in the bag next to it. While I can't seem to stomach a heap of food during the day, in the middle of the night, I'm craving weird things. After judging the crisps—too crushed to salvage—the cheese—been out of the fridge for at least five hours now, and slightly squishy—and the chicken bone—what? I stole some barbeque chicken and ate that in the middle of the night too?—I throw them all in my trashcan.

My phone buzzes on my nightstand, and I reach over to grab it.

> **Michael: Happy Christmas, doll! Hope you get spoilt rotten. Maybe we could catch up tonight? I'm in town seeing Mum before heading off to Wollongong next week.**

I shake my head. God, do I want to. But I can't. I just can't.

I delete the text, as I did the other five messages he's sent me since we returned from Sydney. He's so sweet, and caring, and *perfect*. Why does he have to be so goddamn nice and caring when I've been nothing but a dismissive, whorish bitch?

I throw my phone across the room. Sometimes, it's the easiest option.

Downstairs, the house is buzzing. Mum is bustling about in the kitchen, and a mixture of garlic, onions, and some kind of roasting meat comes wafting up the stairs as I walk down. My stomach gives the tiniest of flip-flops, but my food stays in its place and I smile. Small mercies.

On the couch, dressed to the nines and with a full face of makeup, is Shae, with my brothers Sean, Steve, and Scotty littered on the floor around her. It doesn't matter that Sean and Scotty live out of home—they're still at our house first thing every Christmas morning. Sean's wife, Sally—yes, he managed to find someone whose first name started with S—was even sprawled out on the floor, her baby bump swelling.

I rub my own stomach self-consciously. Sally's not wearing any makeup, but her cheeks are flushed in a healthy looking way, and despite the big round turtle she has strapped to her stomach, she doesn't look as if she's gained weight anywhere else. I wonder if that's how I'll look when I'm at her stage? Will I be the stereotypical "glowing" mother-to-be?

"You've put on a little weight." Shae nods in my direction, and I freeze. Honestly, maybe a tiny bit, but no more than what I would have if I'd eaten a big meal.

I rub my bump again. It's not even a bump. More like a … slight incline and decline.

Ah, crap. That's a bump.

"Just been eating lots since school finished." I shrug it off as if it's no big deal, but mentally bump up *tell family you're pregnant* on the importance level on my to-do list. Because that'll be a fun conversation.

"Keeping in shape is important," Sean says. After getting his masters in business and a diploma in physical education, Sean now owns a gym. He should know. "Are you binge drinking, by any chance?" He looks down his long, pointy nose at me, and I smile. We've never been close—at thirty-two, he's a hell of a lot older than me—but he likes to put on a fatherly display every now and then. You know, when he's not too busy downing protein shakes to waste his open mouth time on talking.

"Not really." I smile sweetly.

"That is one of the biggest causes of weight gain. It makes

you eat the most ridiculous things at the most ridiculous hours of the day."

I smirk, thinking of the chicken carcass and weird snacks in my trashcan upstairs. "I'd believe it."

"I've been on this new diet. I'm basically going all-natural." Shae puffs out her chest. "My boss, Evan—the really fabulous one I've been telling you about—he's been great. He even bought one of those microwave ovens so I can cook things fresh."

"He single?" I smile.

"Has to be," Scotty chimes in, and we exchange a look. The look that says, *"Shae is getting laid by her boss."*

"As a matter of fact, he is married with a two-year-old kid. And he happens to like me for my business skills." Shae levels us with a glare of her own, only hers says *"Unlike you, Scotty Still In University and Stacey Doesn't Have A Job."*

"Can we just get to the presents?" Dad asks. He's so softly spoken, I sometimes forget he's even there. Then again, it's not hard to get lost in the sea of voices of the Allison family. I should know.

Presents are handed out, and unwrapped. Shae gets a new skirt suit. Steve receives a voucher for a furniture store—no doubt a subtle *move out of home* message. Scotty is handed a gift voucher for shark diving in Cape Town—he's going to Africa for two months to help build schools for underprivileged children, and plans to stop at Cape Town on the way back. I get a voucher for a nail salon appointment.

"Who's this for?" Sally asks as Sean thrusts a present into her hands. They've already opened their gift from Mum and Dad, another voucher—since Mum discovered online shopping, she's all about the gift certificate—only this one for a romantic weekend away in the Hunter Valley, an hour or so north of where we live. Aka wine country.

"It's for Peanut." Sean smiles, and rubs Sally's belly. I want to barf. I mean, calling their unborn child Peanut? How original!

So why am I crying?

I quickly shove my fist to my eyes to stop the tears. Screw this pregnancy business! I feel like everything is striking me deeper, touching me emotionally in ways it wouldn't have before.

Sally carefully opens the package—she's not the ripping paper type—and pulls out the sweetest little neutral-coloured jumpsuit I've ever seen. It's just so tiny, and fluffy looking, and they're going to put their baby in that, and—this time I do choke on a sob.

"What's the matter, Stace?" Sean asks.

Seven heads swivel and focus in on me.

"It's just …" *Sob.* "… really tiny." My voice gets a little high-pitched, and I try to calm my breathing. This is ridiculous. It's not like me to get so emotional over such a small thing.

I wipe my eyes.

"Must be that time of the month," Scotty says, giving a half smile.

I sniffle, and my tears stop. Quite the opposite, actually. And not having to shove a freaking tampon into my vagina multiple times a day for a week for the next nine months of my life sounds pretty damn good.

"Ah, the pre-menstrual jokes," Shae says. "The curse we must bear for being women with three brothers."

"What's their excuse, though?" I give Shae a small smile of solidarity and she winks at me and ruffles my hair. Her hand gets tangled in one of the knots and she laces it back out.

"Your hair is seriously so long, Stace. Maybe you could try being a hair model or something." She smiles. "You know, especially if you keep eating and putting on the weight. You probably couldn't pull of catwalk anymore …"

She means well. She really does. And I guess it's a compliment. But sometimes, it's tiring being put in a freaking box.

"I'm going to … check my phone," I mutter, standing up.

"It was a joke, Stace." Shae gabs my hand and tries to pull me back down. I shrug her off.

"All good." I flash her a half-hearted smile and traipse my

way back upstairs.

I walk into my room and flop down on the bed. Man, all this pink stuff will have to go. What if I have a little boy? God, where am I going to live? Will I stay here with Mum and Dad, Shae, and Scotty?

Well, Shae and Scotty are apparently moving out soon …

I need some money. I need to get a job. I need a *plan*.

Later, Shae's words still sting like they always do, but the wound is so much deeper because I know it's true. In the last six weeks, I've fallen pregnant, decided to keep the baby but done nothing about considering how it will all work. I really am the *dumb blonde* she talks about …

I walk over to my desk and boot up my computer, then I Google the sort of financial support I can receive from the government once the baby is born. I also look up jobs available in the local area; maybe I will only be able to work in a call centre or something, but at least I'll bemum trying. I'll be trying to support my child.

I spend three hours researching and planning, making tables and charts, calculating what I need to earn and it all points to one thing—I'm going to have to tell my family. Soon.

WANTED
Phone sales driven, unique individual. Own transport a plus. Passion for finance preferred ...

SPIRITUAL SALES ROLE
Are you in touch with your spiritual side? Can you sell, no matter what the demand? Call now for your free introductory course into our self-healing sales program. We teach you the tricks; you earn the tips.

WE WANT YOU
Can you sell? Then we want you to join our sales team of motivated professionals. Great beginners opportunity.

LOVE UR JOB
Do you love love? Then you should work our phones. Sales based on buyer demand. Sexy voice required. Call now ...

WANTED
Someone who loves sales and can perform under pressure. Sales-driven targets with exceptional rewards! Call now ...

MEDIA MATTERS
Do you have an eye for magazines? Can you build relationships and make things work? Call today, for more information on this fabulously rewarding opportunity.

PHONE CALL = $$
Earn easy $$ with this low-risk investment opportunity from Sex Toys R Us. Promote our products to our researched list of interested individuals. Reasonable prices; call now!

HEARD THE WORD?
Have you heard the word that radio sales are the hottest thing in marketing? Pick up the phone and call! Tell us why we should hire you, and we'll let you tell others why they should hire us.

BE IN INSURANCE
Love your job and help protect others as an insurance professional. Phone based sales role. Work flexible hours. No experience ...

COMMUNICATION PLUS
Do you love communicating and expressing your innermost thoughts and feelings? Combine your love of sales with your spiritual self in an animal-oriented role like no other ...

SHOW ME THE $$
Want to know the fastest way to earn money via phone sales? Indulge in others' fantasies to earn yourself cash the easy way. Don't wait! Call today ...

PHONE SALES
Can you sell for money? Want to earn an unlimited income, beyond even your wildest dreams? Then call ...

I blink. All the ads are blurring into one in my head, and I end up drawing up a blanket resume that will fit every kind of phone sales role I can think of. Well, every one bar the sexy kind, that is.

Tears mist my eyes once more, and again my mind is drawn back to Sean and Sally opening the present for the baby. Why didn't I think of that? For weeks I've been promising my small human that I'll get things right as a mother, but already I feel inadequate, once more pipped at the post by my freaking family.

I scrub at my eyes, and bite my lip. *This is something I can make right.*

I visit the online store for Myer, one of the biggest department stores in our area who thankfully, do online shopping. I want this small human inside me to have the best start to life possible.

I buy a tiny little jumpsuit, very similar to the one Sean bought Sally, as well as what looks to be the softest little toy rabbit and some to-die-for booty things that seriously look so tiny, I doubt they'd warm my fingers. My eyes mist over again, but this time, I smile. I can't wait for my package to come in the mail. It's money I don't really have to spend, but it's it. *I'm going to be the best mother ever.* I haven't neglected my small human on its first ever Christmas.

"Stace?" Mum opens the door, peeping her head into the room. I quickly click the Internet browser closed. "Did you want to invite Kate and her family over for Christmas lunch?

"I don't think so." I purse my lips. "Kate told me she doesn't want to do Christmas this year. I think they just want to focus on their … stuff for a while."

"Huntington's sounds like a truly horrible disease." Mum leans her body up against the doorframe. "I can understand them wanting to just shut everything else out for a while."

"Yeah." I nod.

"All right, well lunch is ready in twenty minutes, so I'll need you to come downstairs. And take a shower before you do." She scrunches up her nose. "Do I smell chicken in here?"

"No!" I widen my eyes and position my legs so they're blocking the trashcan under my desk. No chicken bone in there.

"Okay," Mum turns to leave. "Oh! I almost forgot." She digs into her pocket and pulls out a tiny package wrapped in tissue paper. "This was on the front stoop when I went out to bring in the bins this morning."

She hands it to me. This tiny purple package has my name scrawled on top in black marker. It feels flimsy in my hands, delicate. "Thanks."

Mum closes the door and I unwrap the package with shaking hands. What the hell is this?

Inside, there is a gold pendant. It's thin and delicate, just a simple sliver. It's the numeral one. I furrow my brow. What the hell kind of present is this? And who would give it to me?

I wrack my brain but after five long minutes of thinking, I can only draw one conclusion. I know I've evoked a code of silence, but this calls for at least a text.

> **Me: Thank you doesn't seem like enough. Is it because I came first in drama?**

His reply comes less than three minutes later.

> **Michael: And first in whatever you decide to do in the future.**

I press my lips together and try to stop those stupid tears leaking from my eyes again. Gosh, I'm like a freaking tap! Why does he have to be so nice?

They say opposites attract. All my life, I've wondered if that were true. It's in this moment, with the nicest guy I know thinking of me, caring about me—*believing* in me—that I know the saying is one hundred per cent correct.

And that officially makes me the meanest bitch I know.

Ten minutes later, I'm in the bathroom. This is it. Things

are going to change. I'm taking control of my life.

I pick up the pair of scissors from inside the cabinet and take one last look at my long, blonde hair. *Say goodbye, Rapunzel.*

Snip.

The first cut is clean, and a long chunk of my hair falls into the sink. I smirk. I guess there's no going back now.

Snip.

A second chunk of hair falls onto the white basin, honey-coloured wisps marring the white porcelain.

Snip.

Snip.

Snip, snip, snip.

When I finish, I shake my hair from side to side and try and push it up a little, like they do at the hairdressers. I can't help but grimace. Apparently, me taking charge of my life might have been better done in a hairdressing salon. Calling my new style uneven would be like saying the leaning tower of Pisa is pretty straight.

Regardless, I smile. It's nothing that a hairdresser can't fix, and besides—no one said taking control would be easy.

With a grin the size of a banana spread across my face, I waltz my way downstairs, ready for Christmas lunch. Ready to stand up for myself.

"What did you do to your *hair?*" Shae shrieks.

When did she stop loving me and start hating me?

I narrow my eyes. I don't have time for this now.

I'm ready to make a change.

week seven

December 29

FEEL LIKE my life is on hold. Waiting to have my first ultrasound. Waiting to hear back from the zillions of jobs I applied for, so I can try and look after this tiny pumpkin inside of me. Or at least save some money until it's born, anyway.

I want to give this little human inside me something awesome. I want to look after it, and help it grow, and learn, and just … just be there for it. Because it's a part of me.

I'm even waiting to try and finish the scarf I started knitting two weeks ago. Because seriously, this domestic shit is hard work.

The only thing I'm not waiting on is spew. God, do I vomit like a hell queen. I've heard it said before, but they really don't drive this home enough: it's not *morning* sickness, people! It's eat-a-bread-roll-so-I-can-spew-it-up sickness. And heaven forbid you should smell a whiff of seafood.

That's why, when Kate suggested we go to lunch, I pushed for some retail therapy instead. Anything to avoid having to eat and vomit in front of her.

Although I'll have to tell her soon.

God, that day can't come quickly enough. To not be in this alone anymore, to not feel like such a freak—

"I like the first one." Kate interrupts my musings, pointing to the back of my hand that is covered in tiny pink marks, stripes of colour. I blink. It's nothing special. I quickly make a mental note of things to Google later: are you allowed to wear lipstick when pregnant? I mean, I know you're not supposed to dye your hair …

"Really, though?" I hold up the tester tube next to my mouth. "Because I think it might be a little too candy, not enough pink. Know what I mean?"

Honestly, I couldn't give a rat's, I'm just trying to take her mind off her dad, while not divulging the contents of mine, as well as trying to sound somewhat coherent after what I am now referring to as the title of my new part-time job, Applying For Jobs on the Internet. Seriously, every night since I decided I was Stacey In Control—gosh, the name sounds like I'm a Barbie figurine—I've stayed up until well past midnight Googling jobs. After my initial broader search, I've narrowed it down to anything within an hour's driving distance of my house that involves the word "phone" in the job title. I barely even look at the job descriptions, anymore; I figure as long as I get to sit down while I'm chatting away, I can probably work almost right up until baby-time. And since I have a lot of things I need to save for, that's going to be imperative. *If only the interviews would run a little more smoothly …*

So far, my in-person appearances have not been great. After Prospective Employer Number One tried to look down my top, Prospective Employer Number Two asked me what my five-year plan was and Prospective Employee Number Three got a little bit vomited on—*oops*—things were not going so well. I give a quick glance at my watch, and breathe a sigh of relief. I have one more interview later today, but at the rate our conversation is flowing, I have no doubt that Kate will be relieved when I have to leave in the late afternoon.

I stifle a yawn, and try not to stare too long at the baby care section. I can see baby wipes, formula, and some kind of a cream that looks like it could be for diaper rash or maybe cracked nipples. I rub my hand across my chest surreptitiously. My breasts have gone from substantial to super-sized over the past few weeks. I've always loved my boobs so much … It seems a shame that they're going to be ruined so young …

I hold them a little tighter. I hear they're going to sag and then flatten. Maybe I can find a rich man to buy me some implants later in life …

I pick up another lipstick and twirl the tube around between my fingers. Kate looks up at the ceiling, and I all but hand her the gun myself. This is painful. This isn't how we hang out.

I'm going to tell her. She's going through a lot, but I'm sure she'll want to know. Especially since I'm keeping it, and who am I kidding, I can't keep this a secret any longer.

"Kate, I—"

"I was just walking along, thinking that this was one of the most boring days of my life, when who do I see through the window of the pharmacy? Only two of the hottest girls I know." Michael swaggers over to us. Kate blinks, as if he's woken her from her trance.

My mind flashes back to the last time I saw him. Him, showing up and doing something sweet. Me, straddling him on the bench at the drama school, his lips against mine, his hands in my hair, on my chest, his hardness through his pants—

I suck in a breath. He's taking up too much air. *Michael.* What the hell is he doing here?

He leans in and hugs Kate, then mirrors the action with me. The stench of stale beer oozes from his pores like lava. I cough, and bile roses in my throat. He's making me feel physically sick; why the hell do I still want to jump his bones? And then … and then *cuddle?*

"Michael, just because we're out of school now doesn't mean you can touch me." I offer a little laugh. Michael's eyes flash hurt before they reclaim their usual sparkle, and I bite my lip to stop myself apologising. I need to be mean, to keep up this armour. I told him not to come back.

He shouldn't be here.

A wave of the stale booze scent washes over me again, and my stomach lurches. *Please go away before I vomit on you.* "And you smell like a brewery. Gross." I wrinkle up my nose. *Leave me alone. Seeing you makes it harder.*

"Ah, come on, I don't smell that bad, do I?" Michael's lips grin, but I see the flash of hurt in his eyes. *Again.*

"Yes," Kate and I answer in unison.

Be strong, Stacey. He's in a band, with dozens of hot chicks throwing their underwear at him on stage ... He's a virgin ...

"I, uh, thought you guys were supposed to be out of town this week," Kate says.

Yeah, Kate. So did I.

"Oh, yeah, well, everyone else is in Wollongong, but I wanted to come home and see Mum, so I drove back after the gig instead of partying." Michael freezes and his mouth forms a tiny O, and then shuts again. "Not that the rest of the guys are, you know, partying heaps hard. Mostly they just sit around with Lee and Coal, and ..."

Great. They're bonding. It won't be long before I never hear from him again. Problem = solved.

"Michael, it's okay." Kate waves his speedy explanation off. She bites her lip for just a second longer than I'd believe to be casual. "Dave's allowed to go out and party. We broke up. It's how it works."

"Yeah," I chime in. "Kate and I certainly have been." I flip my hair back over my shoulder, puffing my chest out. *I don't need you in my life. You, or your sexy eyes, or your sexy lips, or your sexy-feeling penis. Nope. No sirree, Bob.*

"Oh, really? That's awesome. Because I have a night off and nothing to do, and it'd be great if you guys were heading out. Then we could all go out together, like old times." Michael's eyes light up, and he shuffles his feet. "It'd be nice to chill on home turf, you know?"

I blink. Crap. "Well, we are going out for dinner tonight." I nod, the action as much to convince Michael of the plan as myself.

"Rad! I'd love to come."

My jaw drops so far it hits the white dirty tiles below us. My heart picks up its pace, practically beating out of my chest toward him à la comic book style. What? I hadn't … But he … *Where did he get that invitation from?*

"So, ladies, shall we just meet out, or have a few drinks before, or …" Michael weighs up the options with his hands.

My heart leaps into my mouth. We can't go for drinks! Or dinner. Or anything …

I look to Kate. *Say something!* Tell him no, Kate. *Please.*

A wave of that stale beer scent wafts up my nose and my stomach lurches again and I realise I don't have time to argue over this. I can't be close to him for another second without spewing on his Doc Martens. "Meet out. We'll go to the Thai place in Lakes at eight tonight."

I can't get the words out fast enough. I need a bathroom, pronto.

"Cool, see ya there, babes." Michael winks and waves, then walks out of the shop as casually as could be.

As soon as he is out of our personal space, I focus on breathing, deep, cleansing breaths that sink to the bottom of my lungs and then clear out all the noxious fumes Michael may have led me to inhale.

Breathe in. Breathe out.

Finally, the feeling of impending sickness sinks down a little. I know it's just biding its time, though; that morning sickness is a nasty little bitch.

"Well … that was interesting." I widen my eyes. The look on Kate's face … she's as pale as one of those alien-like models, and her eyes are as round as powder puffs. The poor thing. As much as I regret asking Michael to hang out with us because of *my* impending dilemma, I know things for Kate are much, much worse.

"I …"

"You need a new outfit. That's what you're about to say, right?" I grab Kate's wrist and pull her closer to my side. I've been so caught up in my own crazy, I haven't really been there for her as much as I could. *As much as I should.*

"I guess?"

"Of course you do. We need Michael to report back to Dave how hot you're looking." I charge forward, heading for the store exit. I may have beaten the vomit monster for now, but I know if I don't get to a bathroom quickly, she'll have her revenge.

I glance behind me. Kate is standing stock still, right where I left her.

My phone buzzes.

Michael: Your hair? Amazing ...

Tears well in my eyes. I need to vomit, I'm feeling so much for Michael, I'm worried about Kate, *I'm hormonal and pregnant ...*

"Kate?"

She grabs a tube off the shelf and takes it to the cashier for payment. "You forgot your candy pink."

"Thank you," I say, and throw my arms around her neck. I'm still not sold on the lipstick.

But sometimes you look into someone's eyes, and you see that they're lost. You see that they need something to anchor them, to bring them back down to earth and reassure them that everything's going to be okay.

And then you realise you're only seeing that, because it's mirrored in yourself.

And you wish like hell someone would hold you like that.

Seven weeks. That's how long it's been since I've had this person growing inside me, this tiny human that I've Googled and found out is roughly three centimetres in size right now.

It's strange how something so small can change your life so drastically. Now, instead of spending my summer uncertain of my future, I have a plan.

Ish.

Or at least, that's what I tell myself as I rock up for my fourth job interview in four days, only twenty minutes late after my emergency shopping trip for Kate.

I run my hands over my "You've ruined it, now" (thanks, Shae) hair, and bite my lip. I can do this. I *will* get this job. I *will* support the small human.

Pushing open the door, I walk inside an unmarked building to a white reception desk. Fluorescent lights illuminate the space and showcase every freckle on the woman behind the desk. And she has so many, you could play join the dots.

I walk up to the counter and clasp my hands on the top, smiling down at her.

"May I help you?" she purrs. Her voice is smooth as silk, and kind of … kind of sexy. I guess as someone answering the phone all day, she really does have the skills for the job.

"Hi, my name is Stacey Allison. I have a job interview with Mischa?" I ask.

"Sure, take a seat." The woman nods to a black leather chair behind me, and I turn and sit down. I drum my fingers nervously on the black display folder I have on my lap. Not that it says anything particularly impressive inside; just a copy of some of my most recent school exams, a reference from the guy who owned the local store I used to work at—before he went broke—and a nice note from our year advisor, Mr Hilman, who scribbled down some notes about my talents as cheerleader two years ago.

"Stacey." I look up. One of the most glamorous women I've ever seen struts toward me on what must be at least four-inch heels. She extends her hand, complete with perfectly manicured French-tipped fingers, and I scramble to my feet to take it.

"Hi. I'm Stacey," I say, then bite my tongue. *Yes, you idiot, she just called you that!*

"Sorry to have kept you waiting; I was on a call. Follow me." Her voice is like liquid gold, all melting and luscious, and I wonder if having a soothing tone like that is a prerequisite for working here. I guess this is a sales company … if most of it is done on the phone that would make perfect sense.

I follow Mischa's tight skirt-clad arse to an office down a hallway. She opens the door and gestures to a white leather chair situated in front of a white desk, which has another white leather chair behind it. Everything about the room is white: white-covered pens, white floor, white walls, and even a white statue in the corner, one of those odd ones where it looks like a naked couple canoodling. In fact, the only thing not white is the deep red rose in a slim vase on her desk.

Mischa shuts the door and dances around me with complete precision to a seat behind the desk. I look down at my folder and pull my skirt forward, only to see her kick off her heels and sink her red-painted toes in to the thick white fur rug beneath her. How does she make that look so attractive?

"Thank you for coming in today," she says, giving me a brisk nod.

I open my mouth to speak, but no words seem to come. What's wrong with me? Where have all my social skills gone?

Stace, you can do this. You're good at pretending, I internally berate myself. *And besides—small human depends on you.*

"Thanks for having me." I smile. I offer my folder across the desk to Mischa, who gracefully retrieves it from my grasp. "This is a folder with my resume, and a few letters of recommendation."

Mischa opens the folder and flicks through, giving small nods every few pages. "How old are you?" She snaps the folder shut with a distinct *clack*.

"Twenty," I answer confidently, chin held high, eyes wide open. Something tells me that this woman would not be impressed by my fresh-out-of-school status.

This answer seems to satisfy Mischa, as she nods, and then says, "Let's talk about your experience in sales …"

"I've worked in sales before, for a period of three years."

Part-time, once a week, at the local store. And by sales, I really mean taking money for candy and occasionally mopping the floor. "And I take pride in giving a job my all."

Mischa steeples her fingers together flat against the desk. "And how do you perform when it comes to meeting targets?" Her voice is so sexy, if I wasn't pregnant and a chick, I'd consider jumping her.

"I have a good track record." I dance around the question, and then, deepening my voice in the hope of sounding even the slightest bit hotter than I so far do, I add in, "And I can be very persuasive."

Mischa laughs, a deep, rumbling sound, and I join her. "I like your attitude, Stacey. I think you could fit in well here. Presumably, you researched us before you came in?"

I blink. Yes. I did. Well, I researched that they had a job opening. The company itself? Once I saw the word phone, I thought it wouldn't really matter. To me it had seemed like the perfect job, one where I could sit down all day, keep my feet up, and not stress out the bub. I rub my belly. After all, it's not too taxing to pick up a phone.

"Yes." I smile.

"And you think you can be ... creative enough to fulfil the role?" Mischa asks.

"Yes." I don't hesitate for a second. Even though by now, I'm having some serious concerns about this whole thing. Creative enough? Isn't this just a sales gig?

"I mean, as well as straight sales referrals, sometimes you'll need to do some work yourself."

My mouth opens and shuts like a goldfish.

"Oh, it's fine. You can study, learn as you go along." Mischa smiles, and I snap my jaw closed.

"I came first in drama back in high school," I say. "I'm good at making things up." *Amen to that.*

"Fabulous. I like your enthusiasm, and honestly, being a niche market as we are, we don't get a lot of candidates, so—"

Now, serious panic signals start going off in my brain. A niche market? What the hell is this job anyway? All I know is that it involves phone sales, an easy enough thing to deduce.

Breathe, Stacey. How weird could the job possibly be?

"Stacey?" Mischa tilts her head to the side and narrows her eyes ever so slightly at me.

"Yes?" I squeak. Thoughts rush through my head. What the hell is niche and a little odd? Alligator sales? Sex toys? Mad cow disease vaccinations?

"I asked if you've ever used our services before." Mischa speaks slowly. A slight frown mars her otherwise silky smooth forehead. *Well, that rules out alligator salesperson.*

"N … no." I swallow. It seems the safest answer.

"Right, well, I'll give you a book to take with you today. It's important that you know a few of the basics in case you get someone who wants to consult with you on the very first call." Mischa nods.

My eyes widen. What if this is a phone sex place? What if I'm selling phone sex, and then sometimes, I'll have to do it myself? It sure would explain why everyone's voice here is so sexy and smooth.

"I'm … I'm not really sure how confident I am at—"

"Relax! You came first in drama. You'll be fine." Mischa smiles an award-winning smile, and I swallow. What the hell have I gotten myself into? "I'm willing to take you on for a two-week trial period at base rate pay, and then after that, if it all works out we can increase your wage to normal."

"Great! Thank you so much." I give a weak smile. My stomach gives a little rumble, but I swallow and amazingly it calms down. It must be fate.

"Fabulous. Ask Candy at reception for one of our instruction manuals, and then I'll see you for your first shift on Tuesday." Mischa turns and opens up her laptop—a white MacBook, of course—and starts tapping away. I stand, and walk out of the room, a little unsure of what has just happened.

On the plus side, I got a job. On the down side, I have no idea who I work for. Or in what industry.

I shuffle through the corridors back to reception where Candy twirls a phone cord around her finger. Her long, blonde hair is swept over her shoulder, and I bite my lip. She's repeating a series of numbers to whoever is on the other end. *Well, at least it seems like she's not having phone sex.*

She finally hangs up and turns to smile at me. "Can I help you, sweetie?"

"Yes. Yes please." I nod. "Mischa said I was to ask you for an instruction book, or something?"

"Oh! The guide." Candy wiggles her eyebrows rather dangerously. "So you're going to become one of us?"

Yep. It has to be phone sex. I'm going to be making money to support my child selling myself on the phone. I can't do this! It's like instead of changing my life to become more responsible, I've somehow managed to become less.

"Looks that way," I mutter, because it seems a hell of a lot easier than saying something insulting such as *Well, now that I've realised what the hell it is you guys do, I am not on board.* I had accidental sex once, okay? I'm not a complete skank.

Candy opens a desk drawer and pulls out a thick, spiral-bound book with a plastic sheet covering the top of it. "Study this," she says, thrusting it into my hands. "Learn everything."

"Thanks." I offer a weak smile. "See you soon."

I turn and walk toward the big glass door, pushing it open with the book facedown in my hands.

"Oh, and Stacey?" Candy calls. I spin back to face her. "You can use that stuff in every day life, too." She gives a salacious wink.

I run to the car and unlock the door, the keys not seeming to want to make it inside the lock. What is wrong with me? Why didn't I research the company first?

My heart plummets, and I'm right back where I was when I finished high school. Of course I've gotten a job as a phone sex worker. I can't believe this is the only interview I somehow managed to ace.

I shake my head. I'll just—I'll email them and tell them I'm not interested. I have a baby to look after. I can't be a mother and do this.

It's not until I pull up out the front of the park down

the street from my house that I flip the book over. I plan on throwing it in the bin there, ensuring my parents don't see it. The disappointment … Ugh!

I step out of the car, the weighty tome in my hands, and open the lid on the metal trashcan. I go to toss it in—

And then I see the title.

I haven't just gotten a job as a phone sex worker.

Apparently, I've landed a role as a pet psychic saleswoman.

Dear Small Human,

It looks like I've done it! I've found a job, and I'm going to be able to earn enough money there to save up and buy you all the things you need, like a crib, and one of those fancy prams that you can take on the beach so I can jog in the sand with you, and maybe a tummy tuck for me! (Joking) I am starting to worry, though. I think I'm still covered under Mum's health insurance, but will that cover all my doctors' stuff in the future?

Right now, I'm feeling the pressure. I'm having to … to make some big decisions in life. Sometimes, you really want something, but you have to let it go. You have to realize when things are not going to work. It can be just as important as striving for your dreams

Of course, I'm not talking about you. I can't wait till you're born. When you're born, we're going to do so many fun things. Walks on the beach. Play group with other babies. Swimming lessons.

I'm not silly, of course. I know it's going to be hard. But what isn't hard that's worth it? The best things in life you need to work for.

I can't wait to teach you to read. We can practice with these letters. You'll snuggle up to me, and I'll open a book, and in my lap you'll look at the pictures while I read the words aloud. Sometimes, you'll make mistakes. But you know what? You'll learn from them. Or they'll make you grow.

No single mistake can ruin everything, Small Human. Always remember that.

Mum xx

"What if they don't come?"

"Shush!" I hiss. Now that Kate's new boss, Lachlan, is coming too, she's turned from a bunch of meh to a bundle of nerves.

"Did you definitely give them the right time?"

"Shut up!"

"Are you sure?"

This last question earns Kate a kick on the ankle. Instantly,

I press my lips together. *Get it together, Stace. No need to lash out.*

The truth is, ever since we saw Michael this morning I've felt on edge, as if little thrums of electricity are motoring through my body. He came back.

It doesn't matter.

But he came back.

"Hey."

I look up.

Shit.

He's standing there in a black button-up shirt that skims over his defined body, a pair of black jeans hanging low on his hips. I swallow. *Sweet mother of tequila …*

"I didn't know what you girls wanted to drink, but I asked my sister, and she said sweet and sparkly was the go, so …"

I shake my head, clearing it of the clearly pregnancy-induced lust stupor I've fallen into. Then I stare at the pink bottle of champagne and the six-pack of beer on the table. Crap!

"That's so thoughtful of you." Kate smiles at him, then looks expectantly at me. Because I love to drink. And I love sparkling wine.

But right now, I'd really just love to vomit.

"I guess we can always walk home." I plaster on the widest grin I can muster, and flag over the waitress who pops the cork and returns with two champagne flutes for us. Kate pours, and the pale pink-coloured liquid fizzes into the glasses, the white head frothing over the top. It looks so tempting, so fresh, so cold … I shake my head. Am I really gonna be able to do nine months of this? Whoever said you don't want to drink when you're pregnant is just full of shit. I wonder if I can try the champagne-behind-the-ears osmosis trick …

"So, is it just us tonight?" Michael slides into the booth next to me, his brown eyes widening. He sits close, close enough that I can smell him. Soap, and beer, and some kind of fresh cologne. I lean a little closer, and take a big sniff … So delicious …

What the hell am I doing? Has pregnancy turned me into a crazy lady who sniffs people?

"No, Kate's friend Lachlan is coming, too," I sing, and Kate shoots me a filthy look.

"Where's Lachlan from?" Michael asks.

"We just work together." Kate studies the paper napkin folded into a crown in front of her. "That's all."

"He's a bit late." Michael picks up the green laminated menu from where it rests in front of him. Gosh, that smell ...

This time, I catch myself before I start licking his neck.

I look up, and there in the doorway is Lachlan. Kate's Lachlan. "Speaking of ..."

Kate looks over to him, and you'd swear we were in a movie and the world slows down, the spotlight resting firmly on those two. Their gazes lock, and I start to feel a little uncomfortable. They're having eyeball-sex, for sure.

"Hey mate." Michael jumps up, his arm outstretched. "I'm Michael."

"Lachlan." Lachlan smiles. "Hi Stacey. Hey Kate."

The way he says her name, the way their eyes connect once more ... seriously, it's enough to make me want to buy Kate a whole pack of condoms for the trip home. I'm so freaking happy for her. After that douche Dave, and her family issues, she needs someone to look at her like that. And maybe to screw her brains out.

"Hi Lachlan," I say. "Why don't you slide on in over there next to Kate?" I point over to the other side of the table, smirking when I feel a sharp kick landing on my ankle. She'll thank me for it later.

Lachlan sits, and the poor guy has barely had a chance to slide his long legs under the table—nice looking, I should add—when Kate opens her mouth. "We should look at the menus."

"Oh, come on, Kate, Lachlan just got here," I say.

"There's no rush." Lachlan shrugs. Kate's shoulders seem to drop just a little, and I smile again. I like this guy.

I pick up my own menu and study the list in front of me.

I seriously need to check out that website on what pregnant women can and can't eat. Seafood seems like it would be bad …

I glance over as the waitress delivers two steaming-hot bowls of red curry to a table next to us. The scent of milk and fish oil curdle together and lay attack to my nose. My stomach churns, and I clutch at it, trying to settle it from the outside.

"Hmm … I think I'll have the chilli basil. I feel like something spicy." There is no way in hell I'm letting anyone else at this table order curry. I squint my eyes, and send what I hope is *Don't eat the red curry* vibes out.

Yep. Pregnant and crazy.

Michael's phone starts to ring, and he grabs it from the table as if it's his secret lover calling, and he doesn't want us to see. He frowns and stands up, taking a few steps toward the front of the restaurant. "'Scuse me."

"Well, there goes his chance," I mutter darkly, purely for show. I know Kate is giving me *hit-on-him* eyes, and this is the best I can do. Then I start thinking of how true it all is, how I am about to get fat and pregnant, while he's on the road, women throwing themselves at him like lambs to the slaughter.

The thought hits me like a freight train. What if he isn't a virgin anymore? What if my last brush-off was enough to push him over the edge, sending him straight into the arms of some waiting wannabe groupies?

Images flash in my mind. Lips pressed up against Michael's. A pink polished-hand running through his thick hair. My chest tightens, and I reach up to place my hand over my heart. It hurts; I'm in physical pain at the thought of him with another girl.

I lower my hand and place it over my stomach. Over my pint-sized bump. *I'm doing it for you.*

"Date not going well?" Lachlan says in a hushed voice. "He seems nice enough."

"He is," Kate says, giving me the death eyes. I pick up my glass of wine and take the world's tiniest sip. It's like drinking glitter. How is it only five weeks since I've been off the drinks?

Anyone would think I have a problem.

"Sorry, guys." Michael strides back over and slides into the table next to me again. Where I wish to keep him. "That was just Dave."

Silence.

Michael cracks his knuckles.

I look over to Kate, and her face has gone the sort of white that ghosts would envy.

"You know what we should do?" Why are there words coming out of my mouth? "Take a photo. Kate, Lachlan, squeeze together."

It's a lame enough ploy, but at least it brings some colour back to my best friend's face.

"Let's not." Kate shakes her head, and deliberately leans farther away from Lachlan and closer to me.

"Why? It'll be cute." I pout, already planning about six good hash tags to go with it. #WayHotterThanDave springs to mind.

Kate bites her lip. "I just don't think it's really appropriate, I—"

"Well, look who it is."

The voice cuts through the air, loud, harsh, and cruel. I spin in my seat.

"Dave. Hi." Michael's face looks as if someone has smashed a pie into it.

Dave slouches, one arm resting up against the dark leather of our booth, the other wrapped around one of the hottest chicks I've ever seen. Of course, I immediately recognise her.

Lee Collins's ex-girlfriend.

Cripes, Michael is gonna pay for this.

"Who are your friends, baby?" the bimbo asks in some sort of European accent, twirling a lock of her honeyed hair around a finger. It's like I'm watching some kind of bad SBS movie. I freeze, unable to stop the horrid things happening around me.

"You know Michael, right?" Dave pulls the girl even closer, so their bodies meld together. "And these are just some girls I went to school with; Stacey and Kate."

As he says the word *girls* Dave flashes his green eyes over at Kate. Rage seethes inside me, boils in my veins and the frozen spell snaps.

"This is Lachlan, Kate's—*friend*." I make no bones about what I mean by that, raising my eyebrows at him.

"Oh, hey man." Dave jerks his head in Lachlan's direction.

"Well, this is a weird coincidence, but I guess I'll just see you tomorrow?" Michael studies his cutlery, which is probably a good plan, since he'll need it for self-defence when I attack him with my chopsticks later. Why the hell did he tell that douchebag where we were?

"What? You gotta be kidding me! Four old friends running into each other on a night like this? We should share a table." Dave opens his arms wide.

"You remember you two are in a band together, right?" Kate snaps.

"Yeah. You're going to see him tomorrow," I say, mentally high-fiving my best friend.

"True." Michael shrugs, his eyes still on the table. Yep, that's gonna be it. Death by cutlery.

"All the more reason to join you now." Dave unleashes his girlfriend from his grip and sits down next to Lachlan, leaving Euro Whore hovering awkwardly next to the table. Dave nods to the seat next to Michael. "Sit."

"Does she respond well to other commands, too?" I purse my lips.

"Yeah. She's particularly good at one *special* command that I know *some* people wouldn't ever do. Am I right, man?" Dave looks at Lachlan, his mouth a wide grin.

"I don't know what you're talking about." Lachlan meets Dave's gaze, holding it without waver.

"You know ..." Dave gives him a not-so-subtle wink.

"No, I don't."

"Well, maybe you guys aren't at that stage in your relationship yet." Dave laughs and runs his tongue over his teeth. "Don't hold your breath waiting, man."

Kate turns red, then white, then this strange in-between blotchy colour. I reach my hand under the table to squeeze her leg, but she moves away. No doubt the memories of the night when she tried to give herself to him are still way too fresh.

My mind is a blur, trying to think up a witty comeback when—

"Huh." Lachlan shrugs, and takes a long swig of the beer Michael had placed in front of him earlier. "Guess you mustn't have been all that good at foreplay, then."

"From what I hear, he certainly wasn't," I chime in. This Lachlan guy—he's growing on me. "A bit of a non-event, you know?"

"You are talking about the bedroom, no?" Dave's accessory opens her mouth for the second time.

"Yes, dear." Michael sounds as if he is speaking to a child.

"Oh." She nods thoughtfully. "He very good and—how you say—fast?"

"She means, like, fast at it, not *quick*," Dave says, but it's too late. We laugh, we laugh so hard that people at nearby tables start to give us worried looks as the implication of his lack of longevity in the sack sinks in.

Kate's face has returned to a somewhat normal colour, and I notice she's shifted slightly closer to Lachlan. Not a lot, maybe not even ten centimetres, but *enough*.

And sometimes, that's all you need.

"Fast and hard, and lasting all night. You know it, baby." Dave stands up and walks to the opposite side of the booth where he bends over and kisses his Swedish miss. And by kissing, I mean opening her mouth, shooting in his tongue, and trying to reach her vagina the long way.

I catch a few girls at another table snapping some not-so-subtle pics. *Not long till you're on a blog somewhere, Dave.* I smirk. I wonder how Lee Collins, the lead singer of the band Dave is supposed to be touring with—and, *oh yeah*, this chick's ex-boyfriend—will feel about that.

"Chill, man." Michael shoots Dave a look, but I wave him off.

"Let him do what he wants. Who cares?" I shrug. Honestly, if they want to force their gross public display of affection on everyone in the restaurant, that's their business.

"We certainly don't, do we, babe?" Kate places her hand on Lachlan's shoulder, and it's almost comical to see how fast Dave stops playing dentist.

"Not at all." Lachlan grins and rests his forehead against hers.

That's when I know.

There, in that moment. That's what I want. I want that connection, that intimate look you share with someone where the shittiest things can be happening around you, but then they cease to exist.

I'm so glad Kate's found that.

And I feel a blow, heavy and low in my gut, knowing that it'll probably never happen to me.

Fingertips brush my leg, and I know Michael has seen it too. We trade a furtive glance. He squeezes my knee.

My stomach flutters, and this time it's not from the need to be sick. This time, I think it's ... holy shit, have I got butterflies?

"I don't know how you do it." Dave stands up and swaggers his way over to Lachlan and Kate, sitting so close to the guy he practically bashes their foreheads together. "You know; put up with all that shit."

"What are we all going to order?" Kate lifts her menu, not making eye contact.

"I mean, you must have a really easy-going family." Dave tosses his head back and laughs, like it's the funniest joke in the world.

He's not ...

He wouldn't ...

"I mean, how would your family react if your girlfriend's dad was going crazy?"

He did.

The words are far too loud. Not only does our table fall silent, but several around it do, too.

"He's not crazy," Kate whispers. Her eyes, they're saucers.

Her cheeks … they're clouds.

"You should have seen him at our graduation. Rocking up drunk, embarrassing the school. And you know what they say: like father, like daughter …" Dave leans over and takes a swig of Lachlan's beer, slamming it back down on the table so hard that the foam rises to the top. "Thanks, man."

Someone at the next table drops their fork. People at the end of the restaurant clink their glasses in a *cheers*.

"A hereditary disease? You're one helluva guy for sticking around for that." Dave rests back in the chair.

Sometimes in life, time seems to slow down. The white foam from the beer still sprays in the air, tiny droplets abseiling down the sides of the bottle and sliding to the table below. Michael's menu gracefully falls from his hand and swan dives its way to the floor. Kate's heart is casually sliced in half by a dancer with a rusty sword.

"Excuse me, guys, I'm just ducking to the ladies room." Time snaps back as Kate stands up and pushes past Lachlan and Dave, forcing her way outta there.

I put my hands on the table to push myself up, but Lachlan reaches across, wrapping his arm around my wrist.

"Stay," he commands.

I have to admit, if I were Kate right now, I think I'd prefer to be comforted by those—my gaze roams—yep, strong, tanned arms than my own.

"Let me know she's okay, yeah?" I ask, grabbing Lachlan's phone from his hand and pressing in my number.

"Course." He takes his mobile back and all but runs out the door, leaving Dave, Euro Whore, Michael, and me.

Well, this is … *nice*.

A waitress walks past with another of those damn curries. Vomit lurches up my throat.

"What the hell is your problem?"

I blink. It's not me talking, for once.

It's *Michael*.

"I mean, you break the girl's heart, she's going through a tough time, then you come here and ruin her night—ruin *our* night, just so you can feel superior about yourself?" His words aren't loud, but they're laced with an anger so seething it is almost tangible.

I'm surprised.

I'm *impressed.*

"And seriously, dating Lee's ex? That's a good career move for us?" Fire flashes in his eyes, and mirrors itself in my body. I'm … I'm turned on by this? What the hell?

"Her name is Inga," Dave spits. I burst out laughing. "What?" he snipes. I almost choke on my tongue.

"I'm just … I'm beginning to think seriously about their offer, man." This time, Michael's voice is quiet. My ears prick up.

"Offer?" I slide my hand across the leather seat, searching for his leg under the table. It's those damn butterflies. They've taken over my wrists.

I find his leg. I squeeze it.

I *shiver.* God, he has some muscles …

"Lee's bass guitarist is leaving, and he mentioned it to Michael," Dave scoffs. "And Micky boy is acting like he's asked him to join as a replacement."

The vomit is back, lurking in the back of my mouth.

"And … did he?" I ask slowly.

"Yes," Michael says.

Michael says *yes.*

The waitress walks past with another bowl of milky curry.

My lunch decides it's had enough.

"'Scuse me." I stand, throwing my legs over Michael's and bolting outta there as fast as I can to the public toilet Kate and I were in earlier. I stumble into the nearest cubicle and drop to my knees, my bones smarting as they hit the floor, and then I proceed to vomit my guts up. The acidic taste burns my throat, lingers in my mouth, and as it happens, I wonder why the hell people stick with this pregnancy lark and why someone hasn't invented a cure for this sickness part yet.

I stare at the pieces of my stomach in the toilet bowl, not daring to move lest it induce further retribution. I think I'm fine. I think I'm—

"Shit!" I shriek, and more comes flooding out of my mouth.

I am so not fine.

"Stacey?"

I slowly raise my head from the floor. I'm on my hands and knees, my hair a mess around my face. Michael probably didn't hear that ... did he?

"Stace, are you okay? I thought I heard ..." I can all but see Michael shuffling his shoes.

I remain silent. There's no way he can know it's me in here. Yep, I'll just stay quiet and he'll leave and then I can go home.

Clunk. Clunk. Clunk.

I shuffle my hands to spin around and shut the cubicle door, but it's too late.

"Stacey." He drops to his knees, cupping my face in his hands, as if I'm some princess and he's in a romance novel. Those freaking butterflies are back with a vengeance. I need to buy some pest control. "Are you okay?"

"Me?" I squeak. "Yeah, I'm fine, just feeling a little ..." *Pregnant?* "... sick."

"Here." Before I can protest, Michael's hands are under my arms and he stands, lifting my body up with him like I'm a ragdoll. His caring eyes bore into mine, light flecks of gold visible in the harsh fluorescent light of the toilet.

"Let's get you some water." Michael half carries/half walks me over to the sink and turns the faucet on full ball. The water hurries out like a train, and he splashes his hand under the stream then catches some droplets for me, raising his hand to my lips. "Drink."

We're close, so close, my arm on fire from his touch, his eyes burning with this strange glow. The water in his hand has slowly escaped through the cracks in his fingers.

With shaky hands, I pull his wrist closer to my face and slowly, ever so slowly, run his pinky finger horizontally through the gap between my lips, flicking out my tongue to lap at it.

His eyes glaze over, and I feel as if I am on fire, as if there's a burning in my body that needs answering. I take my other hand and wrap it around his neck, pulling him closer, staring at his lips, and …

I just vomited.

Oh, ew. Ew, ew, *ew.*

What must he think of me?

"Stacey," Michael says my name, and something inside me breaks. I can't kiss him. I taste like vomit.

I can't kiss him. He could soon be a member of one of a Grammy-award winning band. He's a virgin. I'm pregnant. He's everything I'm not.

He's … Michael.

Tears prickle my eyelids, and I kick myself mentally for letting my thoughts go there. Like it matters. It's just Michael. Michael, who always has been and always will be my *friend.*

I hate how dirty the word sounds.

Except now Michael is wiping his big, calloused thumbs under my eyelids, carefully pressing away the tears I didn't realise had eventuated.

My hormones are out of control! Stupid pregnancy.

"You okay?" He gives this gentle smile, and God, as if my heart doesn't break.

"Mmhmm." I nod and smile.

"Virus?" he asks.

"Mmm." *Yes, the kind of virus you get when sperm implants itself in your egg.* "I'm just really tired. I think I'm going to go home."

I take one step forward then another, Michael by my side the whole time, his hands hovering, ready to catch me if I fall.

Ready to catch me if I fall. I hate to like the sound of that.

We reach my car and I open the door and slide behind the wheel. On the plus side, at least I hadn't had to fake any more of that booze drinking, meaning I can now drive home suspicion free.

"Are you okay to drive?" Michael asks. The moon plays havoc with his cheekbones. It carves them into lust.

"Fine." I nod. "Just tired."

"Ha! You're acting like my mum did when she was pregnant with my sister," Michael scoffs. "She'd throw up, cry, be tired ..."

Sometimes in life, the world gets so quiet you can hear a pin drop.

Now is one of those times.

I open my mouth to speak, but it takes too long for the thoughts to travel from my brain to my lips. Michael's eyes balloon up, as if someone is inflating them with the world's slowest air pump. I drop my car keys, and they flitter to the base of my car.

"You're freaking *pregnant?*" Time speeds up again for the second time tonight. Now the hurt, anger, and sadness are flashing across his face all at once.

"Yes." My voice is a mouse.

"What the fuck? To who?" Michael runs his hands through his hair, paces back and forth the length of my car. "*Why?*"

"Well, when a penis and a vagina—"

"Shut the fuck up, Stacey." Michael pounces. He's all up in my face and I gasp for breath. His words are harsh, but his eyes ... they're glassy. Too glassy.

I'm not Stacey In Control anymore. Now I'm Destruction Barbie.

Michael's breath heats my face. "Why did you do this to me?"

A car whooshes by on one of the lower car park levels. A group of guys laugh somewhere on the street. Still, this space stretches out between us.

Seven seconds. One for each shot of tequila.

"Michael, I'm sorry, I—"

"Just, save it, okay?" He steps back. My words are whips. "I have to ... I have to go."

He turns and walks away, his retreating form spotlighted by the streetlights. The soft rolling of small waves onto the lakeshore is the soundtrack to his departure. A gull cries somewhere overhead and it's lonely, so lonely.

"So that's it?" I bite my lip. I knew he only liked me for what he thought I represented. What he thought I could be. It would never have worked.

Never.

"You know what hurts the most?" He spins around. A couple walking past look at us, then hurry on their way. "You didn't even *try* us, Stacey. You just put us in the too-hard basket."

"You had a girlfriend!"

"Stop, with that. Stop." He shakes his head. "Six months ago. You could have tried."

I swallow. "I … I want …"

I don't know what I want.

"We leave for the States in a fortnight. Maybe …" He throws one hand up in the air, and I don't know if he's saying we'll talk then, saying goodbye or flipping me off. Maybe all three.

I'm hit with another wave in the stomach, but this isn't butterflies or pregnancy sickness.

It's heartache.

And I have no idea why it happens down there.

week eight

January 4

FIVE DAYS, fourteen hours and fifty-two minutes. That's how long it's been since I last heard from Michael.

They are the numbers I work out as I stagger from the car back into the building with the perfectly white walls and furniture, designed in a minimalist style so as "not to detract from the pureness of one's psyche", as Candy tells me, when I ask her about rules for or against pink fluffy pens. (There's no reason I can't try and make work fun, right?)

Despite that frivolity, I'm not particularly thrilled about being here. I've lied to my parents, told them I have a job at a call centre—well, okay, it's not exactly a lie, but I still don't feel happy about it. Honestly, I'm not particularly happy about anything, especially since Michael found out the truth. It feels like each minute, each second has slowly, slowly ticked away. He hates me. He's leaving.

Each time I picture his face, it's like a knife twists further into my heart.

"Okay, now everybody, I want you to imagine your toes. Feel them relaxing, melting into the floor ..." Mischa starts, and I shift my weight, trying to concentrate on my toes. I'm staring at the stark white ceiling, my back comfortably supported by the thick, white yoga mat I'm lying on. Because yes, here at Power of Pets, we have a daily mediation session to begin work. It helps us open our minds, and sets us up for a productive day ahead.

Or in my case, it gives me an extra twenty minutes to think of Michael's face as he accused me of not trying. Michael's words when he found out I was pregnant. Michael's feet as he walked away. "*Why did you do this to me?*"

They're words I may never forget.

"Stacey? Are your eyes open?" Mischa's face pops into view, her pink lips a pop of colour.

"Yes," I mumble.

"This is meditation. How will you ever open your mind and further explore your psychic abilities if you don't participate properly?" she tuts, tilting her head to the side. "Now close." She brings her hands down and trails her cool fingertips over my eyelids, effectively shutting them herself. I shiver.

"Let the relaxing of muscles travel up your body, your calves, your thighs ... your pelvis ..." I snort. Relaxing my vagina seems weird. Luckily, Mischa ignores me. "Your stomach, your shoulders, right down your arms, then up your neck, until finally, you're relaxing every muscle in your face."

I try to de-tense my lips, my forehead, my eyes. It's tricky, especially since as soon as I relax my eye muscles, my stupid lids want to spring back open. I sigh. *Focus.*

"Now focus on white light. On nothing. On empty space." Mischa drones, and I picture a white, pulsing ball of light in my mind.

Michael, wiping away my tears.

No! White pulsing light.

Michael, his arm around me helping me walk.

White. Pulsing. *Light.*

Michael, holding my baby ...

This time, I shake my head. Michael wouldn't do that. I'm pregnant, he's a good guy, he's in a rock band, and he basically told me he hates me; why on earth would he consider being in my life? The list of cons just keeps getting longer.

Pain throbs in my heart again, in my stomach, in my head. It's so hard to shut it all out.

When meditation is over, I breathe a huge sigh of relief. Making calls, I can do.

At least that's one thing I'm going to get right.

"Hello, is this Mrs …" I look at the name on the sheet in front of me, and decide to take a stab in the dark. "Mck-in-liar?"

Silence.

"Hello, is this Mrs—"

"McIntyre, not McInLye."

Damn it! Not for the first time this morning I curse whoever wrote these names down on the spread sheet. Firstly, for the fact they chose to collect hand-written data, versus digital. Secondly, for the fact that their Ts clearly look like Ls. And thirdly, because I know I'm about to make my eighth non-sale of the day. And it's not even one p.m..

Yep. When it comes to selling pet futures, I suck. I suck puppy … fleas, or something.

"My apologies, Mrs McIntyre. I'm calling today on behalf of the Power of Pets, Australia's number one spiritual pet consultancy company in Australia. You signed up for our newsletter at …" I squint a little, trying to decipher the handwritten word in the box next to her name. "… the Pet & Animal Society Show. And wrote that you don't mind us contacting you in the future. Speaking of, how is little …" Pause, try very hard to decipher next boxed word. "… Buttons?"

It's hard to keep the question out of my voice. Luckily, it kinda goes with what I'm saying.

"Buttons …"

Silence.

Did I get the name wrong? Oh, God. Surely I haven't insulted this woman twice in two minutes! It's one thing to mistake a surname, another entirely to get the name of a crazy pet lady's pet wrong. Trust me, until you've met a truly crazy cat or dog lady, this sentence wont make sense. But once you have … well, you're on your own.

"Bottom?" I screw my nose up and give it a try. It's seriously the only other thing I think the scribbled word could be.

"Pardon?" Mrs McIntyre asks, suddenly sounding far sharper.

"Your … dog?" I've gone from certain she's a crazy canine lady to replacing her as a crazy cat one. God, they should list this stuff on the form, as well as a 1–10 scale of nuts to measure them by.

"He … he died. From cancer." Mrs McIntyre makes a choking sound—some sort of a relative of a sob—and my heart goes out to her. "Can you put me in touch with a psychic now?"

I blink. I know that Mischa has already left on her lunch break, and I don't know any of the other girls' names, let alone if they'd consider giving up their lunch breaks for a random client. Especially since opening the conversation involves a woman who is now actively sobbing, her broken wail a continuous cry for help.

I look at the corner of my very white, very shiny desk and pull the phone an inch away from my ear. Although gosh, if I can't handle a grown woman crying at me, how will I cope with a baby?

"Okay, the next available appointment in the system is tomorrow afternoon at three p.m.; does that suit you?" I ask, clicking through the calendar on my screen. In all honesty, I can see six appointment slots free tomorrow; but I think poor ol' Mrs McIntyre needs less choice in her life right now, not more.

"You can't just … can you do me now?"

I suck in a breath. This is exactly what Mischa had tried to train me for. She'd said that sometimes, people just didn't want to wait. They wanted security. Reassurance.

Love.

And they wanted it now.

Still, I wasn't ready to give it.

"You're better off waiting till tomorrow. I can get—"

"I want you to read my pet's spirit, and I want it now! Is that so hard to ask? It doesn't have to be long, and I'll pay double." I suck in a breath. I do need the cash … "Triple!"

"To be honest, I'm not really qualified to do this …" I trail off, but even as I do, the "admin" email address pings and I click open an email from Mrs McIntyre, a photo of her beloved Buttons inside.

"Did you get my email?" she asks. I hit *zoom*. Buttons is a very cute, very fluffy looking Maltese. Or, was, I should say. *Poor Buttons …*

Ping

Another email comes through. This time, Buttons is wearing a tutu. Yes, a tutu. *Oh, God …*

"Look, I'm going to be honest with you. While I have some psychic ability"—It's not technically a lie. In my first training session, post-meditation this morning, Mischa praised me for my efforts, and said I did very well—"I am by no means an expert, and couldn't guarantee you a correct reading."

"Can you just … try?" Mrs McIntyre's sobbing sounds more desolate, more alone, and that's when I know. "If you can't, I'm going to Puppy Power."

I suck in a sharp breath. Puppy Power are our biggest rivals, and Mischa hates them with a passion.

Maybe I could give it a go. I stare at the picture of Buttons again, and then follow the instructions Mischa gave me. First, clear your mind, as if in meditation. Then, picture the animal in question. Imagine them, let them roam free in your thoughts, in your mind …

Try as I may, Buttons won't come to life. The closest I can come is picturing him spinning around performing ballet in that ridiculous tutu.

"Mrs McIntyre—"

"Yes?"

She needs this. I make up my mind. I look at the little timer on my desk that Mischa has told me to hit, should I ever start a consult with a client. It's so she can work out how much to bill them.

I move my computer screen so it blocks the little clock. I can't do this for money.

"Mrs McIntyre, Buttons misses you very much. You two had a very special bond," I say. I look at the picture again. It has to be true. No self-respecting dog would allow its owner to dress it up in hot pink if it wasn't true love.

"Yes, yes he did!"

He? Interesting.

"He's in a better place now. A place with … bones, and balls, and—"

"Buttons is terrified of balls!"

"Ball terriers. Bull Terriers. Who he is friends with, and they're super friendly," I try to cover. "The point is, he knows you miss him, and he doesn't want you to forget the special time you shared together … But he doesn't want you to mourn his loss forever, either." I swallow. "You're a strong woman, Mrs McIntyre; you can get through this."

Silence.

"Th … thank you," Mrs McIntyre says, her voice shaky. "It means so much to hear you say that."

"That's fine. Also, there's no charge for this call."

"You are just a godsend, dear," Mrs McIntyre sniffles. "Do you have a dog?"

"No." I shake my head.

"Kids, then?"

I rub my hand over my stomach. "I'm about to have a baby, though, yes."

Mrs McIntyre sucks in a deep breath. "You will make a fabulous mother, dear. I feel it in my waters."

I stifle a giggle as I hang up the phone, and try not to think dirty thoughts about Mrs McIntyre's waters. I smile. I may have lost Michael—but at least I have this.

"I didn't know you were pregnant."

I whip my head from my desk to see Candy leaning against the doorframe.

"Please, don't tell ..." My words trail off. Who would she be loyal to? Her boss, or the new girl? It's not really a hard question.

Candy lopes across the room and perches on the corner of my desk. "Is that why you took this job?"

"You can tell I'm not that ..." I roll my hand in the air, "... into it?"

Candy sighs, and a blonde lock flies over her shoulder. "Sweetheart, Mischa is one of the kindest people I know. If you haven't told her, I'd say she's guessed. She helps people, Stacey. It's what she does."

She blinks, and her eyes radiate compassion. I manage a smile.

"How are you handling the pregnancy?"

I bite my lip. How am I ...?

"Well, to be honest, I'm freaking out." The words explode from my mouth before I can stop them. "I haven't told anyone yet, and I have no one to talk to, and sometimes I feel so alone, you know?"

"You're not alone." Candy's hand is warm when she places it over mine. "But you need to tell your family, at least."

That lead feeling in my stomach strikes me again. Yes. Yes, I really do.

"But in the meantime, wanna talk about it?" Candy gives my fingers a gentle squeeze. "We can do some seriously good baby fashion research over lunch?"

I smile. I'd really like that.

January 7

Eight weeks, five days. That's how long it's been since I fell pregnant. Which means I have roughly thirty weeks to go.

I'm starting to feel better about it all. I've marked out what cot I want to get, and researched the best stroller for my needs (a three-wheeled one, mind, so I can run on the sand with the kid in an effort to lose post-pregnancy weight). I've booked in my next appointment with the doctor for my first ultrasound. I've even started meditating at night, now that I've learned a few techniques. Apparently, meditation is great for pregnant people. Who knew?

And I've decided that this is the week when I'll tell my parents. It has to happen sometime, after all.

Despite all this, despite the fact that every day seems to slowly inch itself along, like a council worker on a paid-by-the-hour job, I still miss him.

Eight days, thirteen hours and twenty-one minutes.

That's how long it's been since I last heard from Michael. Not that I'm counting, or anything.

And that's how long it is since I've last seen Kate when Mum gets the call.

I know it's bad because I'm sitting on the couch, slowly stuffing one plain cracker into my mouth after the other, knitting discarded on the floor, and all I can hear from the kitchen is, "Oh … oh … I'm so … Oh."

"Stacey." Mum walks into the lounge room and I sit up straighter, brushing the crumbs from my black tank top. "Something terrible has happened."

She sits down next to me and I wrap my arms around my stomach. "Yes?"

"Kate had a friend … Lachlan? He was—he was in a motorcycle accident. He died."

I blink.

Lachlan? Nice, supportive, funny Lachlan?

Kate.

I bolt up off the couch, run to my room and grab my handbag. I have to go to her. I have to go to her now. I—

"Stace, her mum said she doesn't want visitors." Mum appears in the doorway.

I push past her. "It's my best friend. He was pretty much her *boyfriend.*"

I take the stairs two at a time, somehow managing not to fall over my own feet, and grab my car keys from the hall table before wrenching my car door open, slamming it shut, and hightailing it out of there quicker than a wasp on the hunt.

I pull up out front of Kate's house and fly to her front door, my fist raised and ready to give it the knocking of a lifetime, when it really hits me.

He's *dead*.

I suck in a deep breath. My head pounds, and it seems a little hard to breathe. Once more, that whole fragility-of-life thing hits me. How could I have contemplated killing my three-centimetre worm-child when this grown-up man just got taken?

"I'm never going to let anything happen to you," I whisper as I rub my stomach again. I'm going to protect this tiny human from everything.

I knock again and the door opens and I'm still standing there, one hand in the air, one on my stomach, one small breath of air in my lungs.

"Stacey," Deborah, Kate's mum, brings me in for a hug, and I let one arm drape around her neck. I pull back and look at her, really look at her, for the first time in quite a while.

Her once-auburn hair is now streaked with delicate lines of grey. The lines around her eyes are deeper, and the purple that shadows them is unmistakable. You can see how much things have changed for her—it's written on her face.

"Are you … okay?" The word seems so trivial, so *not enough* for what she is going through with her husband's disease, but it's all I have.

"Kate's not doing well, she's—"

"Are you okay?" I put my hand on her arm. "With your husband … Kate …?"

A sheen mists over Deborah's eyes. She's a woman I've always referred to as a second mother, and the next thing I know she's in my arms, her frail body shaking as sobs choke from her mouth. I rub my hand up and down her back, shushing noises coming from my mouth. Comforting her like

I would a baby.

"I'm sorry." Deborah finally pulls back and runs a hand under her eyes. Even though she's in a work uniform, with some foundation covering her cheeks, she's not wearing mascara, so it's just the damp she's brushing away. I wonder when her days started getting like that. So tumultuous that the risk of wearing eye-makeup just wasn't worth it.

"It's fine." I shake my head. And it really is.

I think of my life. Pregnant. Alone. Then I think of her life. Her husband is sick, can barely put together a sentence. Her daughter could die of the same disease. But right now, Kate is in the throes of heartbreak because the guy she really liked has died.

Maybe everyone is alone, to a degree. Maybe I just didn't see it before.

"She doesn't want to see anyone," Deborah says. "It's not just Lachlan, you know. Last night, Dave released a song about her. Some mean thing about … well, I'm sure you'll hear it for yourself."

Anger boils in my veins. "How could he?" I hiss. But what I'm thinking is, *How the hell could Michael be involved with that?*

"Can I just see her for a few minutes?" I ask. "I won't—I won't bother her, I promise. I just want to … I want to be there."

Deborah shoots a wistful look into the darkened house behind her. "Okay," she whispers, and leads me in.

We walk into the lounge room, and it really is like walking into a house for the mourning. The heavy curtains are pulled shut, casting the room in shadow. Someone—presumably Deb—has lit an incense candle, so the heady scent of lavender fills the room. It creeps down my throat, choking me, and I stop, swallow, and try to take shallow breaths. Now is not the time to throw up.

On the couch is Kate. Scrunched up balls of tissue surround her, a pile of them on the floor, and a beige-coloured blanket covers her from the waist down. Her eyes are open, and she's staring straight ahead, but she doesn't make any move to signal she knows I'm in the room.

It's the single creepiest thing I've ever seen.

I tiptoe over to her side, clear a space in the tissue debris and sit cross-legged on the floor next to her. "Kate?"

Nothing. Her eyes look straight past me, straight through me, to something I can't see.

"I'm so sorry, hon." I shake my head and lift my hand, combing a piece of her hair back behind her ear. It's damp, and I wonder if it's from excess crying or sweat. Probably both.

"Your mum told me about Dave, too," I whisper, glancing up to check that Deborah has left the room. "I'm going to take his balls, and mince them, and make them into little pies that I'll force him to eat. And don't even get me started on what I'm going to do to Michael."

Kate huffs out the tiniest of breaths, and it warms my face. It's the only recognition I've had from her so far.

"I know Lachlan was special, Kate. I know you liked him—liked him a lot." I swallow the lump in my throat. "But I know you're going to pull through this." I reach up and take her hand, wrapping my fingers between hers. "The thing is, you're strong, Kate. You're the strongest person I know.

"There is nothing I can say to you that's going to take this pain away. Nothing. But I know that in time, it will get a little more bearable. Not a lot, but enough. Enough for you to smile again. To laugh.

"And I have no idea why this shitty stuff is happening to you, but it's going to get better. And I'll be there to help you through it. Me ... and my baby." I whisper the last words, and look at Kate's face to see if it at least gets some recognition.

She still stares blankly at something I can't see.

For twenty-nine minutes, she stares at space, and I gaze at her. Occasionally I stroke her hair back, or mutter a few words about how wonderful she is, how amazing she is, how strong she is, but it's like she's on another planet. It's as if she has checked out of this world, and is existing solely in her own system.

"'Bye, Kate." I stand up and kiss her on the forehead, giving her hand one last squeeze before I let it go.

I walk out of my best friend's house, but I know Kate isn't really there. And for a completely different reason, my heart breaks into tiny pieces again.

I hop in my car, one sole destination in mind. How *could* he? *How could he?*

I pull up out the front and get out of the crappy old vehicle, kicking the door shut with my foot. It gives a sharp *thud* and I feel a tiny bit more satisfied.

I rap on the front door, and thank God, he opens it. I have no idea what I'd say to his parents right now.

"Stacey." Michael's eyes are wide.

"You jerk!" I give his shoulders a small shove, and he stumbles back.

"What the hell?" He holds his hands up in defence.

"You let that dickhead write a *song* about her?" I spit, giving him another shove for good measure. Michael looks over his shoulder, as if checking to see how much peace I've disturbed in the house. He puts his hand on my forearm and gently guides me back toward the door.

"Let's go for a walk."

He shuts the door behind us and steps in front of me. We walk down the street in silence. Well, he walks. I half stomp, then do a few skips to keep up. He has seriously long legs.

When we reach the park at the end of his street, he walks over to the swing set and sits down. I take the one beside him, wrapping my arms around the chain-link ropes.

"I didn't know about the song," Michael says. He kicks some of the sand in the pit below us and it billows around his black shoes, spotting them with white.

"You're in the band," I snort.

"He recorded it without me! I think he knew I'd … well, you know, I wouldn't be happy with it."

I swallow. I guess it's a believable story. "Wait, don't songs take months to get recorded? Wouldn't that mean he did this while we were still in school?"

"Nah." Michael shakes his head. "Coal have a producer with them on the road, so they've been doing a lot of sessions. Anyway, I found out from Lee—the lead singer of—"

"I know who Lee Collins is," I snap. Who doesn't know who Lee Collins is?

"That they used his bass player to do the song, not me," Michael says. His looks down, his long black lashes fanning over his cheeks. There's a sorrow in his eyes I've not seen before.

"Are you … okay?" I ask for the second time today. How would it feel, having something you worked so hard on stripped away from you?

He stares at the tiny grains of sand. Crystal-white, glinting in the sun. "I'm … going to do the final American leg of the tour. Maybe talk to Lee again, see if they still are looking for a new bass guitarist. Hell, theirs is obviously playing around."

I give him one of those little shoulder punches. "You definitely should, you know. You're a talented guy. Coal would be lucky to have you."

He gives me the briefest of smiles.

"Seriously, you should. And then you can help me castrate Dave. Of all the dickhead things to do …"

"At least she has Lachlan."

I swallow. "He … he died."

"You've gotta be …" The silence stretches out. "Shit."

"I saw her this morning. She's not in a good way."

"He seemed like such a good dude. How did he …?"

"Bike accident. Lost control and ran into a tree." Tears prick my eyes not for the first time that day, and Michael reaches over and touches my shoulder this time. But he doesn't pull away. He leaves his hand there, burning into my skin. It feels good, too good, and for one tiny, infinitesimal moment, I think everything is going to be okay.

"So … we need to talk."

Has anyone ever said those words and then followed with good news? I take a deep breath, let it fill my lungs, and then whoosh it all out.

"You're having a baby," he whispers. His hand is still on my shoulder. That's a good sign, right?

"Yep." I nod.

"Whose?" His eyes are like those of a beggar.

"Um … some guy …" I trail off. Guilt teases at the pit of my stomach once more. Or maybe it's the dreaded morning sickness again. Who knows?

"You don't know?"

His hand is no longer on my arm.

Shit.

"It was that night … at the party you guys played. I was drunk, I don't remember what happened … I just remember waking up."

"The day I found you on the street?" Michael's jaw drops. "You said you stayed at a girlfriend's."

"I lied." With every word, the space between Michael and I grows. The air is thicker. The gap harder to cross.

"This … this is the puppy you were texting me about, isn't it?"

I push back on the swing-set, letting the chains cartwheel forward. Sometimes, one word can be the hardest thing part to say. "Yes."

This time it's Michael who sucks in the breath then lets it release, a noise so loud I swear it echoes through the park. He runs his hands through his hair, shaking his head.

"So you're pregnant with another man's baby, and you're thinking you might … keep—"

"I know it sounds crazy, but it just feels like—I'm so freaking alone, Michael. I don't have a career, like you; I'm working in a call centre for a pet psychic, for crying out loud! Even Kate—I know she's my best friend, but she has a career. And I see the way she looks at me, the way everyone does, like I'm just some dumb bitch who is good for some sort of stripper job or working on the dole." I explode. "I don't *want* that. I want someone to love me, and think I'm something … something more." My shoulders shake, my chest heaving. Tears pour from my eyes in an ugly cry that would make someone watching *The Fault In Our Stars* look pretty. "I just want …" Then the sobs choke me and I can't speak anymore.

My swing slows and Michael's arms are around me. He embraces me, holding me close to his chest, and I let it out, let it all out. How did my life become this? Used, spit out, and unwanted …

When my ugly-cry evolves into an occasional shuddering breath, Michael pulls back. I immediately shove my face into my hands, hiding it.

"What are you doing?" He grabs my wrists and tries to pull them gently down. He's possibly going to join one of the most famous bands on the planet. I'm possibly about to show him just how ugly I can be.

No, wait.

I did that five minutes ago, when I told him the truth about the baby's conception.

"I'm hideous. I just cried." I gulp. "I probably have panda eyes, a red nose, and snot all over my face."

My hands fall from my face and I scrunch my eyes shut, feeling as exposed as I've ever been. Even as I think it, I know how dumb that is. How superficial can you get?

"Stacey, you're more than just some dumb blonde," he says. I slowly release my eyelids, and he's right there, so close to me that I can see the faint ghosts of freckles dotting his nose. The kind that the hint of an Australian summer can bring.

"I'm not—" Swallow. "I'm not saying I think that's all I am, but I just … sometimes I feel so alone, you know? Would having someone to love who loved me back really be that bad?"

This time, the silence that stretches between us feels like it lasts a long time.

"I …" He shakes his head. "Stacey, I like you a lot."

I look into his eyes, those eyes I've seen so many times but only really *felt* eight weeks ago. "I like you, too." They're the most honest words I've spoken to him in a long time.

"I want to make this work but—it's gonna be hard, you know? You've just kept a massive secret from me, and we've been talking almost every second day. How can I trust you when you do something like that?"

"I didn't want to lie." I shake my head. "I was just— protecting you."

"Protecting me from something that would directly affect our relationship? From something that would make me feel … make me feel …" His eyes glisten.

I lean closer and press my lips against his. They're firm and unmoving, but I kiss anyway, my own tears falling down my cheeks to mingle the taste of his sweet lips with my salt.

Finally, after what seems like hours, his lips move, and we press against each other, his mouth opening to me. My tongue slides in and his hands run up my back, over my neck, and lace themselves in my hair, his touch firm and deliciously sensual. His chest is hard against mine and I want him, want him so badly.

No, this is different.

I need him.

Need him so much.

His hands fall from my hair and he gently pushes me away, but I don't open my eyes. I don't want to.

When I do, this will be over.

I know it. He knows it.

"So, what do you think?" he asks in a quiet voice, so quiet that the overture of native birds squawking in the background almost hides the sound.

"I think I like you"—I love you?—"but this isn't going to work. You're going on tour, I have a baby—someone else's—"

"I don't need the reminder." Half his lips rise in a smile.

"I just can't see this"—I gesture between us—"being a thing." And it's true. Even if he could move past the pregnancy itself, how could he be my boyfriend when I only saw him once a month? And if he joined Coal, he'd have to move to America, and I'd never see him, and all he'd see were girls who were skinny and hot while I turned into this whale back in his small-town home.

But even as I've said it, I hear a little voice in my brain. It's on repeat, echoing the same two words over and over again. *Convince me. Convince me.*

He blinks and steps back. His face turns from warm to stone in an instant.

"This is exactly the problem," he hisses.

"Wh ... what?" I blink. Where did this anger come from?

"Since we met, I've had a crush on you." His hands ball into fists at his sides. "I've told you how I've felt since we turned sixteen, and don't you dare use the 'I was dating someone else' excuse, because you know I would have done anything to make this work. But not once—not *once* have you taken this seriously!"

"I am taking this seriously! How can you be with me when you might be moving overseas and having sexy fans throwing themselves at you?" I tighten my grip on the swing-set chains.

"Because I've *loved you for two and a half years,* Stacey."

Love ... loved?

"Because I believe in us, and I believe we can make it work. But you—just like you have every time I've tried to tell you how I feel—you play it off, like it's not sincere, like it's too hard—like I'm a fucking joke to you." He throws his hands from his hair to his sides. His eyes flash, dark and sinister.

"Michael, I'm sorry ..." I wrack my brain for more words, but there's nothing left. There is so much I am sorry for. Sorry for making him hate me. Sorry for not trying to see beyond the surface sooner; for not understanding that he really did care, not until it was far too late.

Sorry for making a mistake.

Sorry that this baby isn't his.

Still, I keep my lips pressed together. There's nothing more I can say.

"Sorry?" He laughs, and it's bitter, and hollow, and it's so loud it makes me cringe. "Sorry you got yourself knocked up?" He steps in closer, so he's right in my face, staring hard into me. "Or sorry that for as long as I've tried to be your boyfriend, as long as there's been this connection between us—and don't you dare lie about this now—you haven't thought I was good enough?"

And with that, he turns, his heel kicking up a cloud of sand as he stalks away.

My swing comes to a stop.

So does my heart.

Dear Small Human,

Today, I love you more than I have yet. I know that feeling will be amplified a million times when you're in my arms, and you know what? It's going to be worth it. Everything will be okay because we'll be together.
I'll give you the world, tiny one. Everything I can, and everything I am.

Love,

Mum xx

January 8

Michael's words play over and over in my head, all night, and halfway through the next day. I keep replaying the scene, doing things differently, saying things differently.

I cry, like I'm a dripping tap, the stupid tears falling down my face.

And I question.

I question every little thing I've ever done to Michael, everything I've ever said. When did I start liking him? Loving him?

I think back to that time at the beach, after he found me on the street. Was it then?

Or was it back in school, when we were sixteen, and I caught him writing my name on the wall outside the school hall, trapped in a love heart with his own initials? I'd blushed. So had he.

Was it then?

I shake my head. It doesn't matter when it was; all that matters is how soon I can erase those memories from my mind. He doesn't want me now. He made that much clear yesterday. And it never would have worked between us, anyway.

I turn to my bedside table and open the jar of tablets the doctor gave me, dry-swallowing two of the folic acid supplements. They stick in my throat on the way down, and I almost vomit them back up. Thankfully, I don't. *Please tell me this means the morning sickness is settling.*

"Stacey! Time to go," Mum's voice rings out from downstairs, and I rub at my eyes. I feel so tired, like my lids weigh a ton. When did it start feeling like this?

I pull on some shoes and join her where she waits in the car, Dad in the front seat. It's Family Lunch at the Mall day. Also known as The Day Stacey Finally Comes Clean About Being Pregnant. I feel like I'm already so damn low, there isn't much further I can fall. May as well just get it done.

We arrive at the café and secure one of the tables in the outside seating area. Dad takes one head, and Mum takes the other, as we wait for my three brothers and one sister to join us.

After ordering, the games begin.

"I got a raise this week," Steve says, through a mouthful of complimentary peanuts. "An extra five grand a year."

"Shut up! I got a raise too," Shae says, smiling brightly. "Evan really likes me. An extra ten, though—sorry, Steve." She smirks, and he tilts his head to the side and raises his glass.

"To Shae," he says, and as one, everyone else at the table lifts their own respective drinks and toasts in her honour.

"Anyone else have any news to report?" Dad asks.

"I got a distinction in my latest uni assignment," Steve says.

"The house we have down the coast just got a fresh appraisal," Sean says. "Worth an extra fifty grand."

"Wow." Dad nods. "Impressive. I propose a toast. To—"

"I'm pregnant," I blurt out.

Silence. Six heads swivel to face me.

What have I done?

"Can someone please pass the water?" I say, studying the white tablecloth in front of me.

"That's ... nice," Mum finally says, choking on the final word

"Do we know the father?" Dad asks, head to the side. Like it's an everyday topic of conversation. Like this isn't the most bad-arse thing anyone in our family has ever done.

Scott, Sean, Steve, and Shae are all still staring at me, as if I've grown a second head instead of housing a second human.

"Nope." I shrug.

Dad's knife screeches against the plate. Mum slurps as she takes a sip of her vodka and lemonade.

"I'm thinking of keeping it."

More silence.

"This is not the life we had planned out for you, Stacey," Dad hisses. "We taught you better than this."

"I'm sorry," I whisper, studying the food in front of me. The gravy on the chicken is mixing with the potato mash, till it all looks like a mush stew.

"I'm very disappointed in you." Dad shakes his head. My heart sinks to my feet. And here I was thinking things couldn't get any worse.

"Now, dear, it's hardly like she was going to be a scholar, or a career person," Mum chides. She reaches across the table for my hand, and I offer it. "This is our Stacey. She's never been one for all that."

I blink.

"Yeah! I mean, she'd be an okay model? Or maybe a good supermarket assistant, but that's about it," Shae adds, flashing me her career-winning smile.

"What the hell's wrong with working in a shop?"

"Nothing." Shae shrugs, but I see the knife in her hands. I know it is aimed for my back.

"Exactly, dear," Mum says. She gives my hand a squeeze. "You just—I'm sure you'll make a great mum, better at that than any other thing you could have done."

I'd thought being told off by Dad was the worst low I could feel.

No. No, it turns out that being told I'd lived up to my career high by my mother and sister was the absolute lowest I could sink.

When did they stop believing in me? I think back to the last few years of my life. There's no clear-cut, defining incident— just a whole heap of small indiscretions. Stacey, suspended for smoking a cigarette. Stacey, kissing a guy behind the school hall and getting busted. Stacey, failing math and geography, for the second year in a row.

Stacey, the least important Allison child.

I stare off into the distance, beyond Mum, beyond Shae, beyond anyone in my stupid family. Is that what I'm doing with this? Taking the easy way out? Being safe, not even trying for the things I could potentially be because I'll fail?

Because I'll fail.

I close my eyes, the hot sun beating down on them. There's still time. If I wanted to.

But how can I kill this mini-human when other humans out there are dying every day?

Lachlan.

Is it fair that I kill this child when Lachlan didn't have a choice in whether he stayed or left?

The voices in my head reach a chorus so loud I feel like screaming to shut them up. What the hell is the right answer here? How do I make things right?

I flash my eyes open, ready to speak, to explode, to try and talk to my family about how I really feel—

And then I see him.

Him.

"Oh! There's Evan now." Shae smiles, and pushes back her chair to stand.

I don't have time to see who she is talking about, because I'm too busy jumping from my seat and lunging at the man walking to a table opposite ours.

I'm by his side in less than three seconds, and I shove him, shove at his shoulders hard.

He looks like no one I've ever met, but someone I know well, as ridiculous as it seems. His eyes, his lips, his jaw, his hips … they're all pieces of a jigsaw puzzle I've been trying to fit together in my mind.

Without a shadow of a doubt, this man is the father of my child.

"How could you?" I scream, shoving him again. He steps back into the chair behind him, eyes wide. There's no shock there, though. Recognition, alarm, sure. But not shock. He isn't surprised to see me.

"Stacey." He grabs my fists and pulls them to my sides. I struggle for a second and then let him. "Stacey, let's step to the side and have a chat, shall we?"

It's then that I notice the woman standing next to him, her hands protectively held over the shoulders of a young boy, maybe two or three years old. He has blond hair like hers, but those eyes … they're the exact same green as the man in front of me.

Flash. Me, tripping over the red shiny thing by the front door.

A toy truck.

He's a father.

I shouldn't be surprised. He's obviously got sperm that possesses super-impregnating powers.

He drops my wrists and walks toward the front of the café and like a mute, I follow. I hate that he has a family. I hate that his kid is looking at me like I'm crazy.

I hate that that woman is looking at me like she knows.

"Look, what do you—"

"I'm pregnant," I whisper. The word barely slips from my mouth.

"It's no—"

"It's yours," I confirm.

He tilts his head back to the sky, lacing his hands behind it and sighs. "I was only at that party for ten minutes. Seeing my cousin." He pauses. "Bloody hell."

We stand there in silence for a few moments. I can feel the eyes of my family and his family trained on us, and part of me wants to crumble up and die. Why am I doing this to myself?

"Look, how much do you need to make it go away?" he asks.

"I … I don't know that I want to," I say. This time, when I speak of not killing it, it feels less like murder. More like suicide.

"You have to." His eyes bore into me. "Don't you get it? Look, if it's cash you're after, I've got it. Not just to get rid of it, but for you, too."

"I don't want … it's not that." I shake my head, words failing me.

"How much? Two grand? Three?" He digs in his pocket and pulls out his wallet. He shoves a fifty into my hand. "I'll get you more over time, over a few months, but just …" He glances back over his shoulder this time worry creases his brow. "… just please, don't talk. Don't be a dumb bitch and screw this up."

"You have a wife and a kid, buddy." I poke him in the chest. "Don't call me a dumb bitch."

"Okay, fine. A dumb slut. I was drunk, okay? You threw

yourself at me. What was I supposed to do?" he asks.

"That's not how I remember it!" I say. Suddenly, the night pieces together in my mind. Me, leaving the stage after talking with Michael. Me, staggering over the grass out the front of the house, looking for a cab. Me, sitting in the gutter, my head resting in my hands, trying to work out what the hell I was going to do with my life.

Him.

Him putting his arm around me.

Him wiping away my tears.

I shiver. "You said you were going to take care of me."

"And I did." He smirks, and tilts his head toward my stomach. "Didn't I?"

"Just stop." Those stupid tears rush to my eyes again, and I swallow hard to keep control.

"You were begging for my dick, just like the easy piece of nothing you are." He opens his wallet again, and hands me another fifty. "Here." He presses it into my hand. "Use it to get yourself checked for any STDs." He smirks, and my stomach roils. "And if you dare come near me again—I mean, ever— your sister gets fired."

I blink.

All the pieces of the jigsaw puzzle fall into place.

He is Evan.

Shae looks at me from the table, and I can see it on her face. Her eyes are daggers, her mouth an *O*.

She knows.

I drop the money, and the sunshine-yellow bill falls from my hands.

I turn.

I run.

I run out of the café, through the shopping centre, and out to the car park that spans an area so wide I swear it's four football fields, at least.

The heat is pounding down on my shoulders, the concrete beneath my feet scorching me with each step, even through my flip flops, as I bolt somewhere, anywhere, away from there.

"Stacey!"

I don't turn around. I keep running, running.

"Stacey," she cries again.

I slow to a stop and spin to face her, my hands on my knees, my breathing coming fast and hard.

Shae walks up to me, centimetres from my face. "How could you?"

"Shae, I didn't know," I say, shaking my head. Even as I do it, it seems weak.

"Like you didn't know when my best friend had a crush on you?" she asks. I wrack my brains for what she's talking about.

"Shae, I was twelve." How can she seriously be mad about that? I hadn't even realised at the time.

"And how you didn't notice when you always got the special treatment at home?" A glassy sheen washes over her eyes. Shit, our whole family has a case of the cries today.

"You were allowed to do everything I had to work for," she hisses. "I had to get good grades, stay in on school nights, eat my fucking vegetables."

I widen my eyes. I've never heard my sister swear. She's perfect.

"And you just had it all fed to you, on a plate. Unless you didn't want to eat it." Shae shakes her head, confusing her metaphors. "And now you've slept with my freaking boss, and are having his *baby?*"

"I didn't know …" I raise my hand, but I have nothing.

"You know what?" She puts one hand on her hip. "You really are a dumb slut. You're easy, you're blonde, you're stupid—of course you're pregnant! Really, the only surprise here is that you did actually complete your leaving exams."

She turns on her heel and flounces off. I swear, steam comes from her feet every time they touch the ground, and only partially due to the extreme heat wave we're experiencing.

I crumble to the ground. My limbs feel like jelly. She truly hates me, to the very core. Everything is ruined. Why the hell did I do this? How did I let my life get this bad? This … alone?

The sun beats down and my shirt sticks to my body. My

hair feels like it's glued to my head, and I lick my lips on repeat, the air drying them almost before I can replenish.

I rub my eyes, and I'm crying a-freaking-*gain*. It's the ugly howling sobs from before, only this time I'm on the floor of a parking lot, with families walking past. Mothers shepherd their children closer to them, urging them not to look as their kids ask why the weird lady is crying. Cars skirt to the left to avoid running me over. My chest is shaking, my breath coming in short sharp gasps. It's hard to breathe. How did the air get so thick? How did everything get so effed up?

Michael.

I want Michael.

I want him, but even he won't make me feel better this time. He doesn't want me. Doesn't need me.

I cry harder, till there are no tears, just stupid ugly sobs.

And that's when it hits me.

He never said he doesn't want me.

I straighten my posture just a little.

He said I never tried, never took him seriously, always dismissed him ... Granted, he didn't say he was thrilled with the whole *baby* thing ... but he never said he didn't want me.

I blink, force my eyes open wide. The harsh sun beats down and I squint again, trying to focus. Would that even make a difference? Did he just want me to fight?

I grab my phone from my pocket and dial his number. It rings, and rings, and rings and finally, on the eighth tone, he picks up.

"Stacey." It's a word, and it's not full of hope.

"Michael, I need to see you. Where are you?"

"I'm at the station. Our train leaves in fifteen minutes, Stace." His voice is slightly softer now, and it's all the encouragement I need.

"Wait there! I'm coming." I hit *end*, and I push myself to my feet. I'm so coming.

I start to sprint. I wish I'd brought my own car, but thankfully, the station is only about a—well, I would have said a twenty-minute jog from the café, but I'm hoping like hell it's only fifteen.

I pump my legs up and down, my elbows swinging at right angles by my waist. I get to the parking lot fence, place one hand on the beam and clear it, running again straight away.

The pavement by the side of the main road is hot, and the exhaust fumes of the cars speeding by clog my lungs, making it hard to breathe. It's stifling, but I keep going. I keep running. Because I have to.

Because I have to tell Michael.

I have to *fight*.

I pound the pavement, a stitch in my side sending stabbing pains against my ribs. For a split second I hope it doesn't hurt the baby, and then I keep going anyway. Because no, I don't want to kill this small cell of a human inside of me.

But yes, I do want to tell Michael how I feel.

Because I'm not just this baby. And I'm not just some bimbo. I'm more than this.

And I want him.

I turn and take a shortcut. The sky has turned a dark purple and a few lights sprinkle the sky above me.

I'm running.

I'm running still, only this time, my feet aren't so much pounding the pavement as making it. It's a little-known bush track near my street, I think the one where Kate said Lachlan kissed her for the first time.

And there it is again.

Lachlan.

Lachlan is dead.

I raise my knees higher, pump my arms faster, make the sweat pour from my body more continuously. Fuck life. Fuck the Evans.

Fuck everything.

And fuck how Michael, a guy I've wanted for so long, who I'd put in an out-of-reach box for so long, just suddenly expose his feelings for me when I couldn't reach him? He's a good thing in my life; how did I ruin this?

I. Let. It. Happen.

Shit.

Oh, shit. Oh shit. Shit, Double shit, how did I not see this before? I let him go. I said goodbye. I thought I was freeing him, but maybe … How do you know?

How do you know anything?

I run. I run faster than I've ever run before. Branches scratch my arms, roots trip my feet, and tears streak my cheeks and blur my vision, until I'm this stumbling, crying, beaten-up mess. How have I become this?

The surface if the ground changes, and somewhere deep inside me, I register that I'm running on road. Bitumen, grass, dirt … What does it matter? All I know is that I need to make it to the station before Michael gets on that train.

My clammy arms stick to my ribs as I try and pick up my pace, but I pump all the more faster. I can do this. I got this.

I've got sixty seconds left to avoid making the biggest mistake of my life.

I don't see the car. I don't hear the horn, nor the screeching of tyres.

All I see is white. Then an image of my baby, of what I'd imagine it looks like now.

Then Michael.

Then black.

Flash.

I'm in a car, lying on stretcher. The wail of a siren roars above me and a woman is there, holding my hand, telling me to breathe.

I do.

She smiles.

Flash

I'm being pushed into a room lit way too bright with those hideous fluorescents that make everyone look ugly. People gather around me, and the woman from the ambulance is saying all sorts of words that freak the hell out of me, such as X-ray, and MRI, and suspected internal bleeding.

I flail my hand around until I finally find hers and grasp and tug on it, till she lowers down, close to my face.

"I'm pregnant," I whisper. We make eye contact, and I think hers are bleeding for me. "Please ... please make sure it's okay."

Because after everything, after all this, I still don't want to kill it.

But I know I can be more. I can have Michael, too. If he'll let me.

"What time is it?" I widen my eyes. A machine next to me starts beeping, faster, louder.

"It's ten past six, dear," the nurse says. "Now be a good girl and close your eyes."

I fight. I fight so hard to keep them open. I blink, and I push my lids up, but they weigh a ton, and my hands have turned to stone.

I'm too late. Now Michael will never know.

"The baby?"

"We need an ultrasound, transvaginal now!"

It's ...

Black.

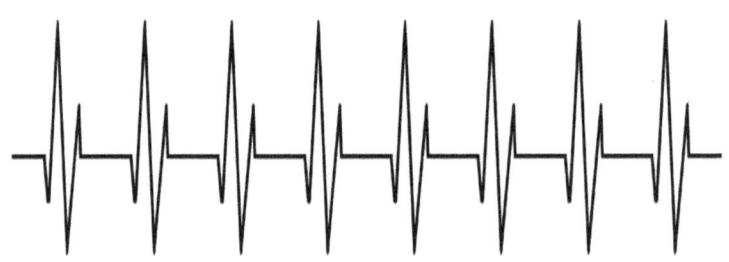

week nine

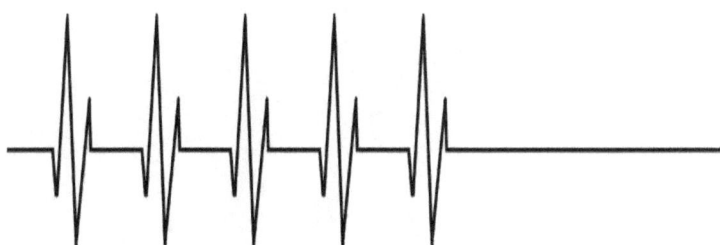

I cried.

January 12

People talk to me. They say things like me being lucky, fortunate, that my injuries are surface.

They don't dig deeper.

They don't see the depth of the wound in my body that is eating me alive.

"It's for the best," Mum says. She and dad have come to visit me, each time with these sad eyes that could speak volumes. They don't, though. They rarely say a word. They pat my hair. They hold my hand. I wish they could hold me closer, try to heal my pain, but they stopped caring for me that way a long time ago.

Still, they come, and when Mum squeezes my arm I remind myself to thank my lucky stars that she's still here.

If only she could squeeze the hurt right out of me.

week ten

January 28

CRY, AND I cry, and I don't stop. I cry for a whole week. I cry when I'm awake. When I sleep, *if* I sleep … I wake up, tears still fresh on my cheeks.

And I'm alone. I have no Michael. No family.

No baby.

I lost my small human.

Everywhere I look, there's a reminder of it. It's in my search history on my computer. In the stupid supplements are still sitting in my top desk drawer.

It's in my hair, the hair I cut so I could try and make a new life as Stacey, the achiever. Stacey, the good freaking mum.

Ha! What a laugh that turned out to be.

"Stacey?" Mum pokes her head inside my room. The light hits her hair, giving her a halo effect. It's the middle of the day, but my room is dark. The curtains stay shut now. I don't need the light.

"This came for you." She places a small package addressed to me at the end of my bed and leaves the room, clicking the door shut behind her as she goes.

I reach over and open the package, wincing as the pain from my fractured ribs shoots through my body.

It's a shiny plastic thing, about the size of half a pillow, and I press against it, the shapes squishing against my fingers.

What in the world …

Then it hits me.

I know exactly what this is.

With shaking hands, I tear open the foil and tip the bag upside down, its contents vomiting onto my legs.

One jumpsuit.

One stuffed toy.

One pair of booties.

I don't know that I can go on anymore.

I cry because I can, for the mean man that Evan is, for his wife and kid who likely don't know that he's a cheater. For Kate, who is still in her self-imposed missing Lachlan exile, hiding in her house.

But most of all, most of all I cry for the little human. My small person.

And then the dam runs dry.

And that's worse than the tears. Because now I have no physical show of how devastated I am.

Dear Small Human,

It hurts, and it doesn't stop. I've failed you. I killed you.
How could I hurt the only good thing I have? I wanted to be your everything, and instead, I deserted

you. I should have looked. I should have freaking done MORE!

I pause in my writing and hurl the notepad across the room.

Everything hurts.

And it just won't stop.

January 29

Me: I know you probably don't want to hear from me. I've left it so long, and I have a reason, but you deserve better than an excuse.

I screwed up.
I'm sorry.
I want to make this work.
I realise that all this time, you were right. I wasn't giving us a chance. I wasn't chasing this, because I guess somewhere, deep down, I didn't think we would work. It wasn't that I didn't trust you, or was ashamed of you; never that. I just didn't think I was good enough. Not for you. Not when you're so smart, and talented, and you have *groupies*, for crying out loud, and I have no career and a baby.
***Had* a baby.**
Had.
I came to see you, that day. The day you left, I was on my way, but something happened.
I got hit by a car.
I lost the baby.

I *broke.*

I want to try, Michael. And this isn't just because I feel like I don't have anything left, and you're the last option.

It's because to me, you are everything. You're the first and *only* option. The only one I ever had, and the only one I know I'll ever want.

And I hope that's enough.

I hit send and stare at my ceiling. I've been doing that a lot this week; with two fractured ribs and a swollen ankle, there's not a heap else I can do.

The doctors say I'm lucky. I'm lucky I didn't do any more serious damage, lucky I didn't get hurt more seriously.

They forget about the scar inside me from losing the baby. The one I'm not sure I'll ever recover from, the one that stings like a knife—that stops me from sleeping. Sleep, that elusive beast, lurks behind the door, in corners, lulling me into a sense of belief that she'll take me, but she never does. Or, if she manages to grasp hold of me, pull me under, it's a brief, teasing embrace that ends with me waking in a cold sweat, flashes of forgotten dreams slipping from my mind. Flashes of the past. Flashes of what the future could have been, if I hadn't screwed it up.

When it's two a.m. and no one else is awake, and it's just me, and my hurt, and the night—the deep, dark, desolate night—it's lonely.

So freaking lonely.

So lonely that when my door creaks open, I shoot upright in my bed and gasp, part from shock, part from the pain caused from the sudden movement and subsequent breath intake against my stupid fractured ribs.

"What the hell?" I screech. My heart is pounding, and I can feel my pulse shooting at my wrist. I shove the stuffed rabbit I've been clutching under my pillow.

"Stace, shut up, it's just me."

I blink at the inky-black figure shadowed in my already

black doorway. "Shae?"

She creaks the door closed behind her and comes to sit on my bed. I inch backwards, leaning against the headboard. "If you've come to kill me, I should warn you that even though my ribs are broken, my lungs are still well in order, and I swear to God, I will scream like a banshee on heat."

"You are such a freaking drama queen." Shae sighs, but there's a smile in her voice. I feel her slide over the top of my feet and rest against the wall to my left, her legs left lying casually over the top of mine.

"So … couldn't sleep?" I ask, after what feels like an hour's worth of silence. Well, okay, a minute. But it's midnight; shit feels long.

"Nope." More silence.

"Shae, I'm sorry about … Evan." I say the name, but even speaking the words makes me feel like my tongue has swollen. I think I preferred it when he was just some faceless guy who'd had sex with me. "It's not like it's any consolation, but I was really, *really* drunk. I … I didn't remember it when it first happened, and now? I kind of have flashes, but that's it."

Lips, rough against mine. A subtle push to his chest. Sucking on my neck.

Pain.

Crickets screech outside my window, the soundtrack to summer by the lake. Our breathing is the underscore, quiet and steady, backing it up.

"I …" Shae shifts her weight, and I feel it on my ankles. "I don't think you're a dumb slut."

The way she says it, so resigned, as if it almost hurts, makes me laugh. Laughing makes my ribs stab against my lungs, though, so it ends up more of a choke. "Gee, thanks."

"You know what I mean." I can practically hear the movement of her rolling her eyes. "I mean … I said some pretty stupid things the other day."

"Don't worry about it." I did some pretty stupid things. "I slept with your boss."

"My *married* boss."

"Your *married* boss," I correct myself. "And … I'm sorry."

"Stace—"

"Seriously, I'm sorry. I was out of control! And I know I've made some stupid choices, and screwed up a whole heap of things, but I didn't mean it. And I'm going to try to make things right." I choke down the sob in my throat, and again, my ribs burn. I wince, leaning forward, which only makes the pain more intense. Seriously, what doesn't hurt a fractured rib?

"Do you remember when you were fourteen? I was eighteen, and I brought Danny home after school that time," Shae asks.

I nod, even though she probably can't see me. "Yeah. Mum and Dad were working late, and we drank some of their vodka, then filled the bottle up with water."

"Yes." Shae's voice is firm, solid. "I took him home, hoping that we would … you know … that we'd …"

"Have sex?" I supply.

"Yes," she says quickly. "But the second he saw you, the second you walked into the kitchen, no matter what I said or how suggestively I said it, he wanted to stay there and hang out with you."

"But I was fourteen." I grimace.

"Exactly." Shae sighs. "Imagine how it feels when the guy who is supposed to be in love with you chooses to hang out with your blonde little sister over having sex for the first time."

I swallow. It's a bitter pill to take.

"And that wasn't the first time a guy had chosen you over me. Hey, even when it came to Mum and Dad, you were allowed to do everything I wasn't. Everything," Shae says. "You could stay at friend's houses when you were fourteen. I had to wait have a guy sleepover till I was eighteen. You went on your first date, solo, at fifteen."

She doesn't fill in the blanks. We all remember Shae's first date at sixteen. The one Dad insisted upon chaperoning.

"The point is, you've always been the pretty, fun, blonde one who gets everything just handed to her on a platter—and I've had to *work*, Stace. I've had to *work*." Shae slams her fist down on the bed, and I feel it vibrate. "And so I guess maybe, I've been a little jealous. Maybe I've been meaner than I needed to."

The crickets continue their overture. My brain starts to work like a rat on a wheel. She doesn't think I—I tried to hurt myself on purpose, does she? "I didn't jump in front of the car, Shae. I didn't see it coming."

"Oh! I mean, I didn't necessarily think you tried to kill yourself." Shae's answer comes all too quickly. "I just mean—I don't think you're a dumb slut, okay? And while I think you would have been a great mum—seriously"—She pauses, and her hand grazes over my knee—"I think you'll be great at whatever you want to be."

She ... doesn't hate me? Her words are full of heart. There's no venom behind them.

Just Shae.

Just my *sister*.

It's been so many years since she's spoken to me like that, that my heart breaks. Tears well in my eyes, and for the zillionth time in the last ten weeks, I start to cry. "The ba"—*Rib stab*— "bies go—o—one," I sob, each syllable punctuated further by a jut of pain. "So why—am—I—still—so—hormonal?" I gasp each word, doubling over in pain again.

Shae laughs, and shuffles up the bed so she's sitting beside me. She carefully places her arm around my shoulders, pulling me close so that my head rests against her neck.

"I love you," she whispers, and kisses the top of my head.

Slowly, my eyes start to drop, the lids getting heavier and heavier, until I can feel sleep pulling at me, trying to drag me under.

"Stacey?"

I fight back to the surface. "Mmm?"

"Just don't do it with my boss again, okay?"

I whack my hand out and hit her in the ribs.

I'm smiling.

And I know she's smiling too.

She gets up and leaves my room. I check my phone for

the time, noting the lack of messages, and I throw it back on my bedside table. I take a little baby-sized jumpsuit out from under my pillow, along with its rabbit friend.

I sleep.

Half an hour later, I jerk awake. My hair is plastered to my face, my breathing short, sharp gasps.

I take more pain medication. I feel slightly better knowing that there's hope for Shae and me, but it's not enough to heal this hole in my heart, this scar that runs deep through my body. Will anything ever be enough?

I swallow the medicine down and it's a bitter pill to take, but it's the only way I can find true relief. It's all I have.

January 30

A long twenty-two days after the accident, I go back to work. My ribs are still a little sensitive, but they've got nothing on my soul. The painkillers are good. They make me feel numb. Numb works.

I don't know why I decided to come here. After all, I don't need the money now. I don't have to save for a crib, or a three-wheeled pram.

I don't have anything at all.

"Stacey!" Candy rushes out from behind her white fortress and embraces me, wrapping her arms around my body.

"Ow." I suck in a breath.

"Sorry, darling," she says, shaking her head. She steps back, her hands still on my shoulders, looking me up and down. "Are you okay?"

Her blue eyes blink. I had already told her and Mischa what had happened to me—well, the CliffsNotes version, anyway. The car accident. The fact that I'd lost my … my small human. It seems such a trivial way to describe what happened, but I couldn't bring myself to talk to them about it all. Not when just saying the word *baby* hurts, like I'm ripping open the wound one more time.

"Getting there." I smile weakly.

"Morning meditation will do you good." She smiles and links arms with me, leading me into the Room of Healing—no shit, that is actually what the sign on the door says—where the other six employees are all stretched out on white yoga mats, Mischa in the centre, holding court.

She nods once and tilts her head toward two empty mats in the corner, which Candy and I promptly take. I inch myself down, slowly lowering my back to try and cause minimal rib discomfort. I can't believe these stupid things can take six weeks to heal …

I ease back and stare at the stark, white ceiling above me. It's so empty. Such a blank canvas. I swallow back another wave of tears. I wish I knew what happened after life; are we alone? Is there a reason for this, for all this excruciating pain? *Is my baby up there, somewhere? Does it need me?*

I choke back a sob. *Please, don't be needing me, little one. I'm no good to you. No good …*

"Now let's focus on relaxing our muscles …" Mischa starts. I try to relax my feet, but my still tender ankle protests when I give it a nudge.

Instead, I jump ahead to the white light part. Just focus on the white light.

White.

Nothing.

Empty.

Whole.

"Stacey …" The word is soft in my ear, quiet, accompanied by a gentle hand on my shoulder.

I blink, and look around. The room is white, full of white light and—*am I dead?*

I blink again. No, the room is just white.

I jolt upright and grasp my ribs, looking around me. Of course. I'm at work. We were meditating.

"Do you need a hand?" Mischa is squatting next to me, a gentle smile on her face.

"Thanks," I say, reaching out and clasping her arm.

We stand up, and I look around again. The room is empty, the yoga mats all rolled away, bar the one I'd just been sleeping on. Through the window, I see the sun setting in a golden yellow beam behind the trees in the park next door.

"What … what time is it?" I shake my head.

"It's six o'clock."

My eyes widen. "Six?"

"Yes." Mischa nods. "You slept—"

"All day?"

"Mmhmm."

I probe around in my mind, looking for the panic I feel when I wake up. Why isn't my breathing short, my throat sore, my forehead clammy?

"I haven't been able to sleep at home. I'm so sorry," I say, then quickly start running through the list of horrible things my boss could have seen me do. Did I snore? Drool? Sleep talk? And *why didn't she wake me up?*

"It's fine, Stacey. A lot of people who go through trauma need to open their minds through meditation to help come out the other side."

Ten weeks ago, I would have scoffed at Mischa's words. Hell, even four weeks ago, I would have giggled.

But now, they make perfect sense.

Now, they seem right.

Because I haven't slept so peacefully in a very long while.

It still hurts, aches, stings like a goddamn bee when I think about it all. But at least my eyes aren't throbbing.

It's a start.

Dear Small Human,

Why?

Please, please don't be needing me right now. I want to be with you so badly, but I know I shouldn't. I can't.

I love you.

Mum xx

February 1

It's been three days, and still no response from Michael. I'm not really surprised. I heard he'd joined Coal—well, I read an article in the local newspaper to that effect—and I guess he is busy being famous, or a rock star, or something. Something more appealing than chasing after the girl who decided too late she couldn't live without him.

Hindsight is a beautiful thing. Looking back, I wish I'd possessed more of it. I wish I'd taken the opportunity when I had the chance.

The pain still throbs in my chest. It feels like I'm floating, existing in this make-believe world, but things are going to have to get real, pretty soon. I guess that's the benefit of hitting rock-bottom. The only place you can go is up.

At least I have something to keep me busy. Kate has organised an art exhibition in honour of Lachlan, so little craft activities have kept me occupied while I've been lying in bed. They've been a godsend. It's amazing how focused you can be when you don't have to *think*. When you don't have to *feel*.

"Knock, knock," I call, rapping on the door.

Seconds later it opens and there is Kate. She's wearing a blue tank today with her black denim shorts. But that's not what changes her outfit, though. It's the smile on her face. It's not a grin; and it's certainly not ear-to-ear. But it's there, nonetheless. I think back to when I last saw her, a little more than three weeks ago.

I drop the box I'm holding and launch myself at her, throwing my arms around her neck as I hold her close, even though my rib is hating me for it.

"You are just …" I shake my head. "Awesome."

She giggles. "Awesome enough for you to quit stepping on my toes?"

"Sorry!" I dance back, and this time I double over as pain shoots through my ribs. Honestly, at least with a broken arm, it would be in a cast. Everything I do seems to set these suckers off.

"Are you okay?" Kate rests her hand on my back and I wince again, trying to pretend like that side of my ribs isn't connected to the side that's quietly trying to play voodoo doll with my lungs.

"Okay," I hiss. "Let's just … go inside." I manage to get the words out.

Kate picks up the cardboard box and stumbles into her lounge room, stretching out on the couch. The curtains are open, allowing the summer light to shine through, and the air conditioner is on, thank goodness. It washes over me in a delicious cooling wave.

"Okay, so I have printed out the labels for the exhibition as requested." I gesture to the box. Of course I had offered to help with Lachlan's exhibition however I could, and hence getting stuck with label duty. Still, we hadn't spoken seriously since ... since everything.

"How are you feeling?" I ask. I lift up her legs and sit down underneath them.

Kate's face blanks to neutral, and I wonder how many times she's practiced the response to this question, or if she's just hiding this part of herself away from me. Away from all of us.

Kate is silent. She shakes her head. "Not ... great."

We sit there for a moment, silently together, miles apart. It's a good kind of quiet. It's one we both understand.

"I'm ... you know, Lachlan's brother, Johnny, he has this so tough. You know both their parents are dead, right? And he's ... he's—" I rub my hand on her back as she hiccoughs down a sob. She presses her forefinger and thumb together as she whooshes out a breath. "I'm fine. He's a really strong person, and he's got it so much worse than I do."

"You're allowed to be sad, Kate," I whisper. "Just because you think he has some worse scenario—it doesn't mean your life isn't pretty average, too. For what it's worth though ... I'm so sorry." And I am. But I know that when it comes to death, sorry doesn't mean shit.

"It's ... you don't have to say that." She pulls her legs from my grasp, but they graze my ribs, and I hiss in a sharp breath, clutching at them again.

"Stace, what's going on?" Kate narrows her eyes.

I press my lips together. I still haven't told her. She's had so much on her plate, I didn't feel right unloading—about any of it.

"Well, um, a few things have gone on." I nod, keeping my eyes fixed firmly on the bright green grass outside of her house. Seriously, that shit looks like it's on steroids. "The most recent being, I chased after Michael to confess my love to him, and I got hit by a car and fractured my ribs."

"Stacey!" Kate launches herself at me this time, and I inhale sharply as she touches my ribs. They're still a little tender. "Sorry! Sorry, ribs, sorry." She flies back, hands in the air, and I have to laugh at the fact that my best friend, whose lover died, who could be facing death herself, is apologising to me.

Only, of course laughing hurts.

Damn it!

"It's … Kate, compared to what you're going through, it's nothing," I choke out.

Kate giggles, and she grabs my hand and squeezes it. "Whoever thought we'd be in a 'Whose life is shittier' contest, right?"

"I know. Do you feel like a Mack Truck ran you over and then reversed for good measure?" I try for a smile.

I earn one. "Like I got pushed off a cliff and then eaten by a whale."

This time, I grin. "Like you got frozen to death, only to have someone set fire to your ice cube?"

Kate giggles, but it peters out into nothingness as she sighs. "It's hard, you know?" She stares into the distance. "Losing someone like that … missing them, it's … it's really hard." She presses her lips together and a tear snakes from her eye. I pull her legs back up and rub her feet, run my hands over her ankles, giving them a soft massage. "I know it must be hard for you with Michael, too."

"Light years apart," I whisper. I know what I'm going through has nothing on her.

"How are you feeling about your results?" I ask. It's four days before my best friend finds out if she's inherited Huntington's disease; if she'll turn out like her father.

Kate closes her eyes, and for a second I worry that she's going to cry.

"I don't think I'm where I was before," she says. I lean in closer to catch her words. "I used to … I used to think it was definitely going to be positive for Huntington's. But weirdly enough, since Lachlan … well, you know … For some reason,

now I'm thinking it could go either way. It could even be …"
She shrugs. "… negative."

"Of course it could." I smile, and I know what she means. Sometimes, it's how humans work. We believe the worst could happen, because when so much bad stuff is going on all around us, why the hell wouldn't it? Why should we be the lucky ones?

A single tear creeps from the corner of Kate's eye and she bats it away with her left hand, shaking her head. "Now, tell me about this Michael business. So …"

I bite my lip. Do I tell her about the pregnancy thing?

I look around the lounge room, at the tissues still screwed up next to the tissue box, the purple smudges still very much under her eyes.

It can wait.

"I just … I won't bore you with the details, but I screwed up. I really liked him, but guess—no, I know I didn't show it," I correct myself. "And now he's all going to be a rock star, or something."

"Coal?" Kate asks, and I nod. *If she's reading the news, she must be better than I'd thought.*

"So have you tried to talk to him?" Kate asks, tilting her head.

"Yep. Well, I sent him a message. He didn't reply."

"Maybe he'd rather say it in person." She shrugs.

I snort. "Yeah, like when? When he comes home next Christmas? Or if I run into him at some party? I'll be there, maybe having landed a gig handing out snacks, and he'll be the rock star coming in to launch the new product, getting paid the big bucks."

Kate shakes her head, and swats me on the arm. "You're not going to be handing out snacks at a party." She settles back into her seat. "Besides, isn't this the year of Stacey? Aren't you just going to take it easy and party?"

Hearing my own words from thrown back at me makes me grimace. Ugh. I'm so far from that person right now. Come to think of it, I don't know that I ever was her.

"No. I have a job working at a pet psychic."

"Ha!" Kate doubles over, mirth escaping from her lips. "You're … you're what?" She screws up her nose as she laughs. It makes me smile. I love seeing her happy.

"Yeah, I know. It's a thing. Pet psychics." I nod.

"Oh my goodness, Stacey! Only you …" She trails off, and looks at the ceiling. "Wait, you're not tricking people and giving them readings, are you?"

"I'm not evil," I say, thinking of poor old Mrs McIntyre. "I mainly just take bookings and make sales. I would never tell someone something I didn't believe was true."

Fact.

"So is this you now? You're a pet psychic booker?" she asks.

I think about it. I think about reassuring Mrs McIntyre that time. About studying the pet psychic tome. About meditating, and taking control of my life. About falling, and trusting someone would catch me.

I smile. It's a bigger than Ben Hur number.

"Actually, I think I want to enrol to study drama teaching."

Later that night, when I'm lying awake in bed, I send Michael another message. I know he hasn't replied to my last one, and this may make me look desperate, but I decide I don't care.

> **Me: So, I hear you're about to be a big famous rock star, or something :) That's awesome. I'm so happy for you. I know you're going to be good at that, and you deserve it. You're a good person, M. The best.**
> **I have some news, too. I've applied for a mid-year intake to get into TAFE. I'm doing a bridging course, so I can hopefully get high enough marks to study teaching next year. I**

want to be a drama teacher. I've even paid for a ten-pack of classes in that acting school you took me to.

What's weirder? I'm actually I little bit excited about it. And Amon even said he'd be *excited* to have me back. You better watch out. I could replace you as favourite.

It's made me think … I don't think I was ready to become a mother. You already know that, right? It wouldn't surprise me. You're freaking smart sometimes.

But I … I don't know that I did.

Well, now I do.

Hope your life is awesome.

I hit send. For weeks, I've been writing letters to people who can't reply; who won't reply.

This time, it's only one hundred and fifteen words. But damn, they feel weighty.

week eleven

February 5

WAKE TO the sound of a drill-saw attempting to channel through a concrete pylon right next to my head.

"Ughhh," I groan. I reach my hand out and slam something in front of me, presumably the drill-saw, most likely the clock radio. Regardless, the action made the noise stop, thank hell.

Hell. While the blast of noise had stopped, there was still a ringing in my head of dizzy-making proportions. Not to mention that my tongue tastes like I've been eating road kill. Yuck.

Harsh yellow light screams through a window framed by black, floral curtains. What fresh hell is this? Who has opened my—

Shit.

I don't have black, floral curtains.

Wait.

Again?

I shoot upright in bed, my heart slamming against my ribs and—

"Surprise!" Mum squeals. I grasp my chest, clutching at

it as my heart does triple somersaults worthy of an Olympics gymnast.

"Wh … what?" I'm breathless all of sudden.

"Well, we thought since our youngest daughter has enrolled to do a bridging course, it was time she had an update to her room." Mum's hands give tiny claps of excitement.

"You got in late last night, and we tried to show you, but you were a little like a zombie." Dad purses his lips.

"Oh yeah." My mind flashes back to last night. I'd stayed up late again with Kate, printing out programs for the guests at Lachlan's showing tonight. When I got home, I'd popped some pain meds and passed out on the couch. I guess at some point I must have seen Mum and Dad and they helped me up to my room, which I now did not recognise.

Instead of the chipped yellow-paint desk, there is a shiny new black Laminex one. My school books have been lined up neatly in one corner, a matching pencil tin acting as the book holder. The tacky stickers have been scraped from the ceiling, and Mum's old exercise bike has finally been moved out of my room, and in its place a long cabinet fronted by a mirror.

"You can put your jewellery inside it." Mum rushes over to demonstrate, opening the cabinet door and showing me all the little slots and hidey holes.

Even my quilt cover has changed. Gone is the hot pink print, and in its place is a plain grey surface. Simple. Elegant. Not ridiculous.

And then, the piece de resistance, the pop of colour in my monochrome style, the black and white floral curtains. Granted, perhaps it was a little unfortunate choice, but they worked, nonetheless.

"Mum … Dad …" Mum clasps her hands together, her eyes bugging out of her head. Dad raises his lips in a half-smile. They look genuinely happy and I'm so very grateful to them in that moment. "Thank you," I say in a very small voice. What they've done … what it means is just … I swallow a lump in my throat. Tears well in Mum's eyes, and Dad has his lips pressed together.

"You know I won't live here forever though, right?" I try and break the tension.

"And?" Dad tilts his head. His spectacles slide down his nose.

"And so it's a lot of work for someone who might leave this town to go to uni," I say, my arm sweeping the room.

"Stacey ..." Mum pauses. "I know it seems like we're not there for you a lot. We were so lucky to have kids who were so ... I guess so self-sufficient, and I ..." Mum's lower lip trembles. "I think I forgot how to be a mum."

I press my lips together. The sight of one of your own parents crying is heartbreaking to say the least.

"Anyway, I know you can't erase some of the things we've done overnight. But ... we're going to try so much harder." She launched herself at me and gripped my hand, pressing her fingers into my palm. "We're going to try."

Big, fat tears welled in my own eyes and I struggled to keep them at bay. "You know I"—sniff—"love you guys, right?"

"We love you too, Stacey." Dad walked over and rubbed his hand against my back. "We love you too."

Dear Small Human,

I'm sorry. I know I've said it before,
but I need to say it again.
I'm sorry for recklessly running across
a road, and ruining your life I put
my heart before yours
God, it hurts I used to read about
people losing babies in the gossip
magazines, and I'd wonder—man,

writing this makes me feel like an idiot—I'd wonder how come they'd get so depressed when their baby wasn't even the size of a DVD case yet. How the hell could I have known?

How on earth could I have not?

I miss you. You know something weird? I'm still taking those folic acid supplements I'm not even pregnant anymore, but it's like I can't give them up.

They're all I have left of being your mum.

I'm going to be okay, though. I'm trying. I think I'll study, become a drama teacher. After all, pretending is kind of my thing.

I miss you, but I know that one day—not tomorrow, not next month, and maybe not even next year—one day, it will stop aching.

I don't think I'll write to you again. But thanks for listening.

Thanks for ... Thanks for everything.

Mut Stacey xx

"Kate." I throw open the door and fly across the room, enveloping my best friend in a huge hug, crushing her arms to her sides in the warm afternoon light.

"How are you?" Kate asks as I pull away, hiding my slight wince from the ribs. Damn, those skinny bones take ages to heal.

"You idiot." I punch her gently on the arm. "How are you?"

"Fine," Kate mumbles. She casts a sidelong look to the left and I see a guy there sorting through a box of prints. He looks nothing like Lachlan, from his blue eyes to his pale skin, but I know it must be his brother, because who else?

I launch my next attack on him, wrapping my arms around him as if we're long lost cousins twice removed in some sort of a country hick movie. He blinks, but ends up patting an arm on my back gently.

"You must be Stacey." His voice sounds quiet, but I think he's smiling. Just a little.

"This sucks." I pull back and look at him, straight in the eye. Because sometimes, "sorry" just doesn't cut it. For a situation like he's in, "sorry" seems like the cheapest word you can buy.

"Hell yeah." Johnny gives a weak smile.

"I think this is a nice idea, though." I turn and look at the art that's already lining the walls. There are black and white sketches he's pencilled out. Images of the beach, the street … lips … Kate's lips? "He was such a talented bastard."

"Stacey!" Kate's jaw drops, and I shrug. I reckon Lachlan would have appreciated it.

"Hey, hey."

That voice.

Michael.

I turn to see him swagger—yes, Michael, *swagger*—into the room. The white shirt he's wearing fits close to his body, the black jeans giving it that slightly rock star look. His chocolate eyes are alive with enthusiasm.

Where the hell did my knees go?

"Michael." Kate smiles and gives him a kiss on the cheek. "Thanks so much for stopping by to help."

I give Kate some serious daggers in her back, which I'm

sure Michael sees. Who cares? It's not like he likes me. People who like you reply to your text messages.

"No worries." Michael nods. "I think this is just such a nice—hey, man." Michael sticks out his hand in front of Johnny who slowly takes it and gives a single pump.

Kate doesn't let the moment last long, instead angling herself so she's facing the two of us. Michael and me.

Oh, no. Surely she's not going to …

"Okay, well, I need you two to go through the guest list and make a check sheet for the bouncers, then sort out a music playlist," Kate says. "But Johnny and I need to concentrate, so I'll need you in the backroom." She gestures toward the little room at the back of the café.

"Do you think I'm an idiot?" I raise my eyebrows. What the hell is she trying to pull? I can't be stuck in a small room with him.

"Nope." Kate shakes her head, and lays her best puppy-dog eyes on me. *Bitch.* "I think you're a good friend who'll do what I ask in my time of need."

Damn it! How the hell can I argue with that?

Michael does his usual energetic walk over to the room and I traipse behind, my feet sticking to the floor.

The back room of the café is as you would expect a back room to be. It's full of boxes of stock, paperwork littered across a desk, and a heap of switches and other important looking things flashing electronically in the corner. The deep scent of coffee washes over me. I wonder if you can get high from this stuff?

Thud.

I spin around. The door has slammed shut behind us.

Bitch.

"No coming out till your jobs are done," Kate shouts through the door.

Double bitch!

I suck in a deep breath, and spot a sheet of paper with names down the side, crosses and ticks in a column next to it. "Okay, so I'm guessing this is the list …"

I pick it up and rifle around the items on the desk in search of a pen and piece of paper so we can create a new sheet for the bouncers. Honestly, why she didn't she just print this out is beyond me …

"You know, you could at least talk to me," I say. My eyes don't leave the list of names in front of me. They can't. "I'm sorry about everything. I'm … I'm making an effort, you know? I'm trying to change."

Once more, I'm greeted by silence. If I hadn't heard him speak to Kate and Johnny before, I'd swear the guy had turned mute.

What a freaking dick, anyway. Who ignores someone, someone you used to care about, when you're locked in a tiny enclosed space together?

I slam the pen on the desk and spin around, my eyes flashing. Only to see … *me*.

Michael has done something fancy with his computer and what I'm guessing is a little projector, because a photo of me is blown up and projected onto the back of the white storeroom door.

In the photo I'm laughing, leaning forward, and even without the glory of high-definition and full colour, you can see my eyes are sparkling blue and that I really am … happy.

"Michael …" I look at him. He's got this small, close-lipped smile on his face, and is leaning back against the counter his computer is resting on.

He presses a button on the computer and soft music starts to play in the background, the gentle strains of a guitar strung along in a nice, easy fashion.

"Stace, you have to know that I wasn't mad about the baby," Michael says in a voice that makes me step closer to hear him better. "I mean, sure, I wasn't thrilled, but you know it's more than that, right?"

"Of course I know …" I silently add *now* to the end of the sentence. I've known since the day in the park, but sometimes, you're so blinded by your own trees, it's hard to see the forest. Or however that stupid saying goes. Honestly, who can be stuck in a grove of trees and not see a forest?

"The thing is, you pushing me away hurt," he says.

"I didn't mean to … I only did it because I didn't think I could be … what you needed me to be." The words come out surprisingly easily. Only once did they get peanut butter-glued to my throat.

"I know," Michael says, and I grin as I catch him muttering "now" under his breath. We are so very similar and yet so completely different. "And that's why I've made you this."

He hits a different button on the computer in front of hum and all of a sudden the soft music changes to "Sadie, the Cleaning Lady", an old John Farnham song that has me bursting into laughter.

"What the hell?"

"Shh!" Michael hisses, and the pictures begin to change.

The first image is me, but not me—it's my head superimposed over that of a woman cleaning a bathroom. She's kitted out in fifties housewife attire, a handkerchief knotted around her crown. Underneath the picture, in bold font, it reads:

You could be a cleaning lady.

"Really?" I fold my arms and give Michael a *look*, but he only laughs. I have to admit, a small giggle escapes my mouth, too. It's pretty funny. And he's freaking *hot*.

And not mad at me.

Next the image changes, and this time it's a picture of what I'm fairly sure is supposed to be Frankenstein, pouring some sort of bubbling liquid from one test tube into another. Again, my face has been superimposed over where his ugly mug would be, with the caption below reading:

You could be a mad scientist.

"Michael." I laugh.

The song reaches the chorus, and the image changes again. This time it's a picture of my head superimposed onto what looks like someone in a swimsuit pageant, mid-strut down the catwalk in a red bikini.

You could be a swimsuit model.

"Now that one really isn't a stretch." Michael winks, and I roll my eyes. But I take a step closer to him. He doesn't move away. In fact he—he reaches out his hand. His deep brown eyes sparkle and I delicately place my hand in the palm of his.

His hand is warm, and soft, and strong. And safe. Lord, his hand is *safe*.

The next slide shows up and every bit of control I just exhibited flies from my body as a photo of a woman cradling a newborn baby in her arms comes onto the screen.

You could be a mother.

"Michael." My voice does that stupid high-pitched thing it does when I'm about to cry and he grabs me, pulling me into his strong arms. I hiccup in a sob, feeling his warmth. It's nice, here in his arms. I blink back my tears. He stokes my hair.

It hurts, thinking about what I've lost.

But I don't feel like I'll be lost forever.

You could be a teacher.

Now there's a shot of a woman writing on a blackboard, her head twisted back to look at the class. Michael gives my hand a little squeeze, and I feel those stupid tears that I swear should have stopped now that all the pregnancy hormones are out of my system, but no. Apparently not.

I quickly form a list of the least emotional things I can think of to try and stem my tears. *Ant farms. Science. Dieting. Shirtless men.* My eyes still prickle. Damn it. This is Kate's event. I can't be a blubbering mess!

Naked Michael.

His body is still deliciously close to mine, and I can feel his chest rise and fall with each breath. One of his strong legs is resting lightly against my thigh. His hand strokes down my arm, and I shiver.

Yep, that did it. The tears are gone.

The final bars of the song start to sound and I take one last look at the screen. This time it's a photo of Michael and me. It's after one of the boys' gigs and—I squint. I'm wearing the clothes I wore the night of the party. The night this whole mess started. His arm is wrapped around my shoulder and he's kissing me on the cheek, his guitar still slung around his neck.

I'm grinning, and a flash of memory hits me. I remember that moment. He'd just finished playing, and a few girls from another school were all over him, no doubt wondering if he'd work those fingers on them next.

I walk over and casually—well, casually would be putting it nicely—place a small kiss on his cheek.

He looks at me, questions in his eyes, and I smile. "You know, I've wanted to do that for a really long time."

He extends his arm and pulls me close, our hips flush together. I look down at our bodies, pressed tight now. We fit. We fit so well.

"So why haven't you?" he whispers in my ear.

"With the band, and my going nowhere ... I could never be the right girl for you."

"Stacey, you're amazing. You know I've had a crush on you for as long as I remember."

"You had a girlfriend!"

"We broke up, but it's because she wasn't ... she wasn't you. And I'm not experienced enough to be your guy, but I want to give us a try, Stace. I just need you to show me you want this enough."

"What do you mean?"

"I'll move heaven and earth to be with you. I'll fly you to our gigs; hell, I'd freaking propose if that's what it took."

I giggle. I do it nervously, because this? This is something I've dreamed of for years. Something I never thought would happen. He's always been in a relationship, and I've floated around, ignoring his flirtatious remarks.

Right now though, the look on his face tells me he's serious. And I couldn't be happier.

"I'm not, though." Michael widens his eyes. "I'm just saying that I ... I love you, Stacey. And I want you to be my girl."

"Stace, Michael, get in for a photo!" Kate shouts.

I blink and focus on the screen again. In big, bold letters underneath the image it says:

You could be my girl.

Michael squeezes my hand, looks into my eyes. "I know you're worried about the distance and everything, but you have to know that we can make this work." He swallows, and his Adam's apple moves up and down. "I mean it, Stace. You can be anything."

Silence stretches between us. My heart races, and uncertainty rushes through me. What about the other girls? What about trying to see each other? Will he have to move to America? Will I—

"Because no matter what, you will always be everything to me."

It's as if all my troubles melt. All my worries melt. All of my spinal cord melts, because my legs drop out from under me and I stagger, Michael's arms lifting me back up. "Will you?"

I look deep into his unblinking eyes.

"Yes," I breathe, and kiss him. Our lips mesh together, our teeth knocking in our desperation, and I pull back. "Yes, yes, yes." I punctuate each affirmation with another kiss, and we laugh, this joyous laughter that has me grinning so hard my cheeks hurt.

"Yes?" He giggles, pulling my body so it's tight against his. I feel his hard chest, his hard length between my legs, and I shudder.

"Yes." This time the kiss deepens, and I open my mouth to let his tongue collide with mine. It's tantalising, full of need and lust and desire. I run my hand underneath his shirt and he's quick to mirror the action with mine. His arm twists and he grips my hipbone, shoving me up against the wall where he cages me in, forcing his body over me, on me, around me.

I breathe, and we're breathing in the same air. He lifts my hands above my head, holding my wrists in place. He's really in control—and I like it. I like knowing that this guy can do anything to me. Because I trust him. More than I have anyone ever before. I will no longer have to run.

Michael's lips lower onto mine I part mine in response, our tongues seeking each other out, finding, exploring. My hands are still trapped above my head, but one of Michael's runs down the length of my body, then slides around to my front, caressing my breasts. His fingers find my nipple through my clothing and I shudder—yes, *shudder*—against him.

He releases me from his grip, and this time both his hands run down my body, then slide up underneath my skirt. Heat pools between my legs, and as his fingers graze over my lacy underwear, I try hard not to thrust toward him. It's as if every nerve ending in my body is alive and on fire, and *ready for him to freaking touch me.*

"Stacey …" he groans into my mouth, and he slides my underwear to one side. I gasp as his hot skin connects with me, igniting me. My knees are weak again, and I wonder how this one guy, this one guy who I've only just—as of ten minutes ago—started dating can turn me on so much? He's even a virgin, and—

Oh. Yeah.

"Michael, I …" I gasp his name out between kisses. "We have to stop."

"Do you really want to?" His hand reaches up to caress my breasts again, and I feel my body move toward it, welcoming his embrace. Damn traitorous body.

"Michael." With a deep breath and willpower I swear, I didn't know I possessed, I manage to push him away, nudging his hands off me. Instantly, I feel the loss of his touch. I have to do this; for him, and for me. But damn it! Being responsible sucks. "Michael … I want your first time to be special."

There. I said it. Michael looks at me, his eyes dark, his lips turned down.

"I know that's weird, but seriously! I do." I shrug, shaking my head. "Well, ninety per cent of me does, anyway."

"Who said anything about having sex?" Michael asks, but I can tell from the twinkle in his eye that he's only joking.

He wraps his hand around the nape of my neck and draws me closer into another kiss. It's sweet, and it's hot, and it's enough. It's a promise of more.

It gives me reason to look forward to tomorrow, and to smile. Yes, I can still feel the pain throbbing through me when

I think of my baby.

But right now, I feel freaking fantastic.

"You go first," I hiss, and Michael shoots me a questioning look before I push him through the doorway and out into the crowd. The doors have opened, and people are flooding in as if someone's just called *sale* in a Sephora store.

He stumbles forward and I smile as he recovers into his usual step, walking up and slapping someone on the back before turning back and winking at me. I can't help the flush of heat that races from my head to my toes. It was a kiss, a few wandering hands …

I give my shoulders a shake.

Focus, Stacey.

I walk out of the storeroom, my head held high, and I know I look like the cat who just ate the cream because let's be honest—I kinda did.

I run my hands over the sides of my hair, attempting to push it back in line, but give up when I catch a glimpse of my flushed cheeks in the window that looks out onto the street where crowds of people are still lined up, waiting to enter.

I race over to Kate who stands in the middle of it all, looking like a gluten intolerant chick at a pasta-eating competition.

"This looks amazing." I grab her elbow, flashing her a grin. I'm so freaking proud of my best friend. How the hell did she pull all this together? "You did it!"

"So, I guess this means you're okay with me forcing you to spend time with Michael?" Kate scrunches up her nose.

"I guess." I narrow my eyes. "But don't let it happen again." I wink, just as an arm wraps around my waist. I shiver, and fall back into him. I trust him. I know he's going to catch me.

"It was that easy?" Kate asks, a smirk lining her face. "I just had to get all *Parent Trap* on you and shut you in a room?"

"Apparently." Michael squeezes my waist, his fingers way too close to my boobs for public consumption, and I roll my eyes. "He's really persuasive, okay?"

He nibbles on my ear, and heat flushes my chest and creeps up my neck.

"Oh, guys! Come on. Gross." Kate shakes her head.

I giggle, and let Michael lead me away, through the crowd of people and back toward the back room.

"You want to make out some more?" I smile. He opens the door and I run my hand sneakily along his waist. Just because we're not going to have sex doesn't mean we can't have a little fun.

"Stace, I—"

"Shh," I whisper as I press him into the storeroom, slamming the door behind him and locking my lips with his. I reach around and pull the zipper of my dress, letting it fall in a pool at my feet as I press my lingerie-clad body against his firm one.

"Stace." This time he puts his hands on my shoulders and pushes me away, then immediately pulls me back close. "Meet Lee."

I blink. I look over his shoulder and there, standing in the corner of the room, right next to the coffee beans and right next to where we just made out, is Lee freaking Collins, lead singer of the Grammy-award winning band Coal. Aka Michael's new band.

"Uh ... hi." Lee smiles, but it's all teeth and no eyes. I jerk my head back and it slams into the door, resulting in me flinging it forward and holding my hand up to apply pressure.

"Ow, ow," I mutter. I drop to the floor to pick up my dress, but Michael comes with me to try and hide my naked-ish body, instead bashing foreheads with me as we go to stand again.

"Shit—"

"Ow!"

"Let me—" He tries to move behind me to zip up my dress at the same time as I try and turn to give him better access, resulting in this awkward getting dressed dance that would make a nun embarrassed.

Finally, we get our act together, and I run my hands over my thighs, then extend one toward Lee.

"Nice to meet you." I smile. Should I curtsey? I'm not really sure on the rock royalty rules.

"Nice to meet you, too." Lee smirks, grasping my hand in his and shaking. I try and pretend like I didn't have posters of this guy on my schoolbooks last year.

"I arranged for Lee to come here and sing as a surprise for Kate and Johnny," Michael says. He looks to the floor, and I grab his hand and squeeze it. It's one of the nicest things he could have done, and I know Kate is gonna love it.

"So this means you sorted things out with her, Michael?" Lee asks, grinning.

"Did you, *Michael*?" I press my lips together and stifle a laugh.

"Whatever," Michael nudges my ribs and grins himself. "Yeah, she came 'round."

"Congrats, man." Lee slaps him on the shoulder. He takes a step closer to me and offers my arm the same treatment. "You should know, he has not shut up about you since the band joined us on tour. I'm hoping now he's loved up he won't be any less hard-working."

"No," Michael and I say in unison. We look at each other and grin.

"I mean, you know I'm super stoked for the opportunity to join Coal," Michael says. He squeezes my hand. "Stace and I will make it work, no matter what."

"Glad to hear it." Lee nods.

Michael looks at his watch and swears. "Sorry, guys. I gotta go get this started. Lee, you ready to roll?"

"Sure thing." Lee smiles.

"Sweet. I'll see ya from the crowd." Michael darts out of the room, and I turn to follow but am stopped when a hand grabs my arm.

"Stacey?" Lee asks.

I turn and face possibly the hottest man I've ever met. Yet I have no desire to screw him. There's only one sexy musician I wanna see naked anytime in my future.

"Don't screw him over." I blink. *What?* "He's a good kid. And dating a guy in a band is hard. Just be in it for the long haul, yeah?"

At least the answer to this question is easy.

"I can be that girl," I say, and I smile.

Because this is one person I know I want to be.

The rest of the night passes in a blur. Kate uses the microphone to say a few words, and then Lee takes the stage and sings this amazing song he wrote, dedicated to Lachlan—"I told him to do that," Michael whispered—much to Kate's obvious astonishment.

The awesome thing was, her dad was there through it all, supporting her, holding her. Loving her.

"It's beautiful, isn't it?"

"Shae." I spin around. Only it's not just Shae. It's Shae, Mum, Dad, Sean, Sally, Scott and Steve.

"We are so proud of your Kate." Mum grabs me and pulls me into her bosom where I choke on her Revlon perfume.

"And of you," Dad interjects. He places one hand on my shoulder.

"Always." Mum smiles. Tears glisten in her eyes, and in that moment I know this is it. This is what I've needed, what I've craved from them for so long—and I hope like hell it's here to stay. I feel like I matter. Like I matter to *them*.

"And who's this?" Shae puts her hands on her hips and looks directly at Michael, whose hands are latched around my waist as if he's afraid I'll float off at any moment.

And I love it.

There's nothing bad about it.

"Michael." He extends his hand and shakes with my brothers and sister. Mum wont accept his offering, however, and brings him in for another hug filled with way too much boob and perfume, and not enough air. I know, because he coughs. Twice.

"My boyfriend," I add, to make sure there's no confusion.

"Congratulations," Steve says.

"Make sure you take care of her, son," Dad says. He folds his arms across his chest, and even though I know I should be mortified, I'm kinda thrilled. Because he's acting like a douche. A douche who *cares*. And I can't argue with that.

"Rain dance."

The words ring out through the room, a screeching, masculine cry over the shrill female voices that are humming to the tune of Lee Collins.

My eyes scan the crowd for the one person I am fairly sure who would be the source of the noise.

Kate's dad.

"Rain dance time!"

He's standing near the door, one hand on the handle, Deborah clutching his arms with her lips pressed so hard together, she could roll pasta through them.

"Come on." I grab Michael's hand and we push through the crowd, trying to get closer to the door.

"Raaaaaain dance." Paul races outside into the pouring rain, his arms spread wide, welcoming the damp.

Voices still as everyone focuses on the man with the disease in the rain. A few cameras flash.

"Hmph! Crazy," a woman says near me, nudging her friend's arm. I give her a right good elbow to the waist. She gasps, and I tilt my head to the side and shrug. Manners, people.

Then something happens that makes my heart explode with pride. Kate grabs her mum's hand, and together they go racing out into the rain, joining Paul there.

Water drenches their clothes, sticking them to their skin.

Kate's hair is plastered against her head, but she has this big, ridiculous grin on her face.

I don't know if she's ever looked more beautiful in her entire life.

"Rain," Paul calls, and he strips off his jacket, letting it rest in the gutter in a wash of dirty water.

Seeming not to care, Kate grabs his hand offers it to Deborah. They share this look so intense, so full of freaking love, that I swear something inside of me melts. Even though they've gone through this crazy illness, this crazy disease, they're still in love.

Michael squeezes my hand. I shoot him a grin.

What was the point in fighting it?

"Kate!"

We're in the doorway before I know what I'm doing, and then we're running through the rain. I squeal as the first drops hit my face, then twirl around, embracing the feel of the warm drops as they land on my skin.

"Woo!" I scream, throwing my hands up in the air, a smile on my face.

I spin and am taken by the waist and twirled through the air, the hands then pulling me close so that Michael can plant a kiss on my cheek.

"We can do better than that," I whisper, grabbing his jaw and pulling it close to my face until his lips press against mine and we're kissing. His tongue pushes its way into my mouth, duelling with mine, and my hands search his back, desperate to feel his well-defined muscles again. The water causes our clothes to stick to us and it only makes it easier for me to feel his erection through his pants, and it somehow makes me want him all the more.

When we pull away I see that Lee Collins is out here too, talking to Kate, and I look over then glance back at Michael and grin.

"Right?" I ask.

"Right." He grins, and there's a look in his eyes that signals that he gets it. He gets how excited I am that Lee is talking to

Kate, seeing how insanely beautiful she is in this moment.

He gets that Kate deserves a second-chance with this guy who Michael clearly approves of, because when you've been friends with someone for as long as Kate and Michael have, you don't let new people walk in and trample over your mate's life.

Michael gives my hand a squeeze, and the look in his eyes—lust, desire, but something more—something like *love*?—it hits me, straight to the core.

He gets me.

And I freaking love that.

I glance at my watch, grinning like a maniac as the clock strikes past midnight.

"You know it's been eleven weeks to the date since I kissed you for the first time?" I smile.

"But it's been five years since I first fell in love with you."

Five years.

Eleven weeks.

A lot can happen in a short period of time: pain, heartbreak, love, loss … and sometimes, something can grow from those ashes. It can rebuild you, heal you in ways you never imagined possible. It can find scars you'd forgotten, rip them open and cover them anew.

That's who I am today. I dove to my lowest low in order to become Stacey, but healed. Stacey, but accepted. Stacey, but loved.

Sometimes, you just gotta let the rain in.

ACKNOWLEDGMENTS

I'd like to thank the Academy, and ... okay, my acknowledgements may not be quite as lengthy as *that* Oscar's speech, but they do have a tendency to go on, so I'll try to keep it brief!

To Kim, my lovely cover designer, thanks so much for your patience with me when I asked if we could try this or that again. Your patience and talent know no bounds, and I love you for it!

To Marion, for editing my work, putting up with my silliness and also, being able to count. Seriously, how'd you get good at words *and* numbers? That just doesn't seem like a fair distribution of talent!

Emily, as always, you make my books so pretty! Thanks for putting in the hard yards.

Before any of these people got to see my book, however, and before I even thought I could publish, I had it beta read. I am fortunate enough to have some of the best and probably most good-looking beta readers going! A huge thanks to Simone, for scaring me then not even being as nasty as you made out; to Kristine, for inspiring me to make a change; to Jennifer, for your awesome notes and incredible turnaround time; and to Stacey because even if I know it isn't true, I love it when you pretend that one day I could be like Colleen Hoover. Who could get better encouragement than that?

To every single blogger who reviewed *The Problem With Crazy*, I cannot thank you enough. In particular, I need to send my utmost love and a zillion unicorns to Kellie, Kristine and Jodie. You all made me cry with your nice words! I can't believe I was lucky enough to have such awesome ladies as you say nice things about me. If you haven't already, you have to check out A.K.A. The Book Harlots Review, Glass Paper Ink Book Blog and Fab, Fun & Tantalising Reads. Seriously, people!

A big shout-out goes to my lovely Chandelle, because I can't remember ever writing a book without bombarding you with a zillion medical-related questions. You're the best fact checker, doctor and friend I know. Love you!

To Mum, Kristy, Andy, Mitch, Marg, Jeff, Lisa, Paul, Scott, Danger and Berry ... I love you all. And humans, come on, stop sulking at sharing your acknowledgment with the puppies.

SydVegas, baby! S, C, JJ and K, you girls make my day, every day. You're always there for me, and I #FLAYFF! Thanks for being awesome, for letting me pretend I can be an editor and an author, for keeping me sane, for giving me advice, and for Batman. And Pringles. Because, der.

Of course, I have to thank my husband (hehehe ... *husband*) for letting me talk about writing *all the damn time*, and for the heart-monitor line. I love making things up with you, and being your wife. You're freaking awesome, and the best thing I have.

Finally, and most importantly, to you. I can't begin to express how stoked I am that anyone would read even a few chapters of my work, let alone a whole novel. Thanks so much for taking the time to check out my work. You'll never know how much it means to me.

aBOUT THE auTHOr

Lauren K. McKellar is a writer and editor of fact and fiction. She loves writing and reading, and hopes her books make you feel *all the things*—or some, at the very least.

Lauren loves to write for the young and new adult markets, blogs with Aussie Owned & Read, and is published both as an independent author and through Escape, Harlequin Australia's digital-first imprint.

In her free time, Lauren enjoys long walks on the beach with her two super-cute dogs and her partner-in-crime/husband.

Connect with Lauren

www.laurenkmckellar.com
https://www.facebook.com/laurenkatemckellar
https://www.twitter.com/LaurenKMcKellar
http://goodreads.com/laurenkmckellar
http://tsu.co/laurenkmckellar

And if you'd like to join my street team, my e-newsletter or even my writing goals group, don't hesitate to email me at laurenmckellar@gmail.com

THE PROBLEM WITH crazy

Crazy in Love #1

The problem with crazy is that crazy, by itself, has no context. It can be good crazy, bad crazy ... or crazy *crazy—like it was when my ex-boyfriend sung about me on the radio.*

Eighteen-year-old Kate couldn't be more excited about finishing high school and spending the summer on tour with her boyfriend's band. Her dad showing up drunk at graduation, however, is not exactly kicking things off on the right foot—and that's before she finds out about his mystery illness, certain to end in death.

A mystery illness that she could inherit.

Kate has to convince everyone around her that her father is sick, not crazy. But who will be harder to convince? Her friends? Or herself?

The Problem With Crazy *is a story about love and life; about overcoming obstacles, choosing to trust, and learning how to make the choices that will change your life forever.*

THE
PROBLEM WITH
Heartache

The one thing he can't forgive.
The one thing she can't forget.

CRAZY IN LOVE #3

The problem with heartache is that you can dream about the could have—the should have—but when you wake, nothing will console you.

Because seconds later, you remember he's dead.
And remembering is the worst pain possible.

Kate is running from her family. It's intertwined with everything that went wrong. When she lost her career. When she lost her sense of self.

When she lost the boy she loved.

Now, she's got a second chance, travelling with rock-star Lee Collins and his band, Coal, on the road. She wants to forget, and she wants to fall in love.

Now.

Lee will do anything for family. It's why he hired Kate.

It's why he donates thousands of dollars every year to the foundation that supports his father.

It's why he keeps his secrets; and it's why he cannot, will not fall in love. Not with Kate—not with anyone.

Ever.

Read on for more of *The Problem with Heartache...*

The problem with heartache is that you can't mourn forever. You can't walk around the streets, wearing black, carrying holy water on your person in the hope that you'll stumble upon a miracle, be able to use it and bring that person back. One day, you're gonna forget that tiny vial, and you're not gonna realise until it's too late.

"Are you done?" Mum enunciated each syllable like it weighed a ton.

"Give me a second." I threw my arms behind my back, fiddling with the straps on the bra.

A solution for heartache, however, appeared to be running. Or, it seemed to be for me. I'd been jogging on the beach every day for six months now, and slowly but surely, I was getting better mentally, becoming able to function again.

Even if it meant that my boobs were getting smaller. Hence the new sports-bra shopping trip.

"Are you having fun?"

I cringed. *Really, Mum? Fun?*

My fumbling finally resulted in success and I shook the bra off, quickly shrugging my normal one over my shoulders and throwing my T-shirt on top of that. It hung loosely over my hips, the grey speckled material suiting my mood to a tee. *Ha. See what I did there?*

Making bad jokes to yourself: a potential symptom of heartache. Thankfully, not a symptom of Huntington's disease.

I grabbed my purse from the little seat the staff at the lingerie store so kindly provided its change room patrons, and walked to the front of the store to the checkout area, sports bra in hand, ready to make the purchase.

The guy in front of me at the counter was taking a really long time. He had six different sets of lingerie to put through. I couldn't help but check around his arm to see what. Black lace, red silk, black pleather … and was that something with fur I could see?

"Stop stickybeaking." Mum slapped my arm, and I snapped my head back to my chest.

"It's a public place," I whispered. The transaction in front of me continued. Hopefully, underwear-fetish guy hadn't heard.

"People don't like you to look at their knickers, Kate." Mum tutted quietly, shaking her head.

"Well maybe *people* shouldn't buy quite so many pairs. And besides," I hissed, raising my eyebrows at her. "We don't know that he's going to wear them all at once."

"Ahem."

Of course. You whisper three fairly innocent sentences, but the one about the guy in front of you being a cross-dressing lingerie wearer, he hears.

"Sorry." I studied the ground.

The man turned around to face me. He had maroon leather shoes, scuffed, like they'd seen better days. My gaze travelled up his black jeans, over his red-chequered shirt with the triangular collar, the black scarf around his chin, covering his lips, his nose—but not his eyes.

Holy hell, did the man have eyes.

"Kate."

I blinked. *What?* How did this guy know my name?

"Yes?" Mum replied, and I jabbed an elbow to her ribs.

"That's me." I smiled brightly. "Sorry about the panties-wearing comment."

"To be fair, this does look a little weird," the guy said. *You can say that again …* "We just have this film clip tomorrow, and the stupid wardrobe guy said the models won't fit any of the … you know …" The man jerked his thumb toward the counter, indicating the underwear the checkout chick had now finished ringing up.

Cogs clicked in my head. This wasn't—

"Lee?" I silently added *freaking-Collins*. If he was going to the trouble of wearing a bad scarf by way of disguise, I doubted he'd be keen on me screaming his full name in a crowded shopping centre.

"Yeah?"

Silence.

"Kate's just so happy to see you, is all," Mum said. She took a step closer. "Hard to recognise, behind that scarf there."

"That's kind of the point." Lee gave her a wink. I swear, my mother blushed.

"Well, we'd love to have you over for dinner sometime, since you're in town," Mum was saying, her hands clasped together. She opened her mouth to continue speaking.

"But being a really busy guy, we wouldn't actually expect you to come." I overlapped.

"Well, if we invited you formally, we would," Mum said, giving me a strange look.

"I mean, I could." Lee spoke the words softly, taking a step closer. "So long as you don't tell anyone about my secret identity."

Mum giggled like a schoolgirl. *Help me, God.*

I looked past her, past the stands of bras and the occasional naughty dress-up item and into the shopping centre and—

Him.

I dropped the sports bra and ran, shouldering Mum as I surged forward, out the doors of the shop.

Left?

Right.

I could just make out the brown hair bobbing in the distance.

I bolted, as fast as my legs could carry me, darting around mothers with prams, old people supported by walking frames, and teenagers making their way to the food court in an achingly slow fashion.

Turning the corner, I could see the hair again, but it was

still too far away. My knees rose higher, my feet hit the ground harder, and I gave it all I had. I couldn't let this opportunity get away. I had to take it. I had to *make* it.

This time when I turned the corner, he was almost within arm's reach. Ignoring the stares I was getting from the lunchtime food-court crowd, I dove, reaching out and grabbing onto the denim of his jeans as I fell.

I hit the ground, hard. Tiles smashed into my ribs, my knee, the side of my jaw. Everything went black for a few moments, and I blinked, trying to clear my vision.

When I could focus again, I looked up. Faces hovered over me, voices yelling things, asking things that I couldn't quite make out.

I need you.

Then I saw him. The blue jeans, the white shirt. The brown floppy hair.

I blinked, and concentrated all my brainpower on focusing on his face. *His face, Kate. Look at his face.*

"Lachlan?"

I blinked again. An old man wearing a chocolate-coloured beret looked back at me.

Shit.